PRESENTED BY:

Van Wert Rotary Club

SOCCER
HALFBACK

READ ALL THE BOOKS

In The

New MATT CHRISTOPHER Sports Library!

CATCH THAT PASS!
978-1-59953-105-2

CENTER COURT STING
978-1-59953-106-9

DIRT BIKE RACER
978-1-59953-113-7

ICE MAGIC
978-1-59953-112-0

THE KID WHO ONLY HIT HOMERS
978-1-59953-107-6

LONG ARM QUARTERBACK
978-1-59953-114-4

MOUNTAIN BIKE MANIA
978-1-59953-108-3

SKATEBOARD TOUGH
978-1-59953-115-1

SNOWBOARD MAVERICK
978-1-59953-116-8

SNOWBOARD SHOWDOWN
978-1-59953-109-0

SOCCER HALFBACK
978-1-59953-110-6

SOCCER SCOOP
978-1-59953-117-5

The New

MATT CHRISTOPHER

Sports Library

SOCCER
HALFBACK

NORWOOD HOUSE PRESS

CHICAGO, ILLINOIS

Norwood House Press
P.O. Box 316598
Chicago, Illinois 60631

For information regarding Norwood House Press, please visit our website at:
www.norwoodhousepress.com or call 866-565-2900.

This edition was published in 2007.

Library of Congress Cataloging-in-Publication Data:
Christopher, Matt.
  Soccer halfback / by Matt Christopher.
      p. cm. -- (The new Matt Christopher sports library)
  Summary: A young boy is pressured by his family to abandon his promising soccer career for football.
  ISBN-13: 978-1-59953-110-6 (library : alk. paper)
  ISBN-10: 1-59953-110-0 (library : alk. paper)
  1. Large type books. (1. Soccer--Fiction. 2. Family life--Fiction. 3. Large type books.) I. Title.
PZ7.C458So 2007
(Fic)--dc22
                                        2006036451

Printed in the United States of America

To sports fans Mose, David, Sam, and Abe

SOCCER
HALFBACK

When the Razorback player kicked it, the soccer ball sprang forward as if shot from a catapult, striking Jabber Morris squarely on the chest. It was a severe blow, and it knocked the breath out of him.

Recovering quickly, he raced after the bouncing ball and dribbled it across the center line into Razorback territory.

Looking for a Nugget target, he saw Mose Borman cutting in front of a Razorback forward. Just then another Razorback player charged at the ball from Jabber's left side, and for a moment all Jabber could see was a blurred green shirt. Then an elbow jabbed him in the ribs, and a hard-muscled shoulder collided with his own, knocking him away from the ball.

He stumbled, but regained his balance in time to get in front of the ball and stop the Razorback's kick.

This time the ball smashed into his knees. He was so close to the kicker that the contact sounded like the one-two punch of a boxer. The ball ricocheted toward the middle of the field where both Razorback and Nugget players converged on it.

"Jabber, you okay?" Mose asked as he came running up to the center halfback.

"Yeah, I'm okay," Jabber answered dismally. "Did you see that Ace Merrill jab me in the ribs with his elbow? And the refs never saw it."

"I know. Half the time those guys seem to be blind," Mose said.

From the Nuggets' bench came a yell that Jabber could identify by now no matter where he heard it.

"On your toes, Mose! Get that ball moving! Come on, Jabber! Up and at 'em!"

Coach Ray Pike was a goal-getter. This was his second year at Birch Central and he wanted it to be better than his first when his Nuggets had won four games and lost six.

"There is no direction for us to go but up," he had said in the locker room just before the team had gone out to the field. "I can't play the game for you. All I can do is teach it to you. Soccer looks simple, but it's not all kick, kick, and more kick. It's a thinking game, too. And that's what you should do out there most of the time — think!"

Jabber sucked in a deep breath, let it out, and ran down toward the touchline where the ball was landing after an arching boot by a Razorback. He stopped the ball with his chest, then got off a good kick that Butch Fleming received and dribbled across the center line into Razorback territory. Butch advanced it a few yards, then booted it to Stork Pickering, the Nuggets' six-feet-three center.

Two Razorbacks converged on Stork. Jabber saw that the tall kid had no one near him to pass to, and that a long kick might just put the ball back into Razorback control. Mustering up speed, he rushed up a couple of yards to Stork's right side, yelling, "Pass it here, Stork!"

Stork saw him and passed it. The pass was good, skidding ahead of Jabber where he got in control of it without slowing down.

Instantly two of the Razorbacks' backfield men rushed toward him. He waited till they closed in on him, then gave the ball a short, quick kick to Mose Borman, who came up running behind them. Mose stopped the pass with his knees, then kicked it back to Jabber, who was running toward the Razorbacks' goal. Jabber, receiving the ball only a few yards away from the Razorbacks' right goalpost, gave the ball a hard, solid boot and sent it flying past the goal-keeper's outstretched hands.

The ball struck the corner inside the net for the Nuggets' first score.

"Nice boot, Jabber!" yelled Mose, throwing his arms around the tall, grinning halfback. "It's time we broke that goose-egg tie!"

Cheers exploded from the smattering of fans standing behind the sidelines and sitting in the bleachers. Jabber looked for Pete, but his older brother seemed to have been swallowed by the small crowd.

Pete had wanted Jabber to go out for football — as he himself had — just because their father had made a big name in football at Notre Dame.

Maybe my performance today will make him change his mind, Jabber thought hopefully.

He returned to his center halfback position, the

ball was centered, and the Nuggets fought frantically to tack on another score while the Razorbacks struggled to tie it up. One minute and ten seconds later the first quarter ended, both teams having worked up a good sweat.

Again Jabber looked at the small crowd. This time he easily picked out Pete. His brother was standing directly behind the time table, wearing dark sunglasses to ward off the bright afternoon sun. Pete waved, and Jabber waved back.

Jabber knew that Pete wasn't here just to watch him play, but to make his own analysis of Jabber's performance. Pete, a running back for Birch Central's varsity football team, hadn't had a chance to see his brother play yet.

The second quarter moved along as swiftly as the first, with the ball shifting into Nugget territory, then back again into Razorback territory.

The quarter was about two minutes old when the Nuggets began to threaten again. Stork stopped a long Razorback kick with his chest, then booted it to Rusty Hammond, a forward. Rusty, a little guy, dribbled the ball a few yards, then passed it to Jabber. Jabber moved it toward the goal, evaded a

Razorback player by a quick shift of his feet that did crazy things with the ball, then got within scoring distance.

Just as he brought his foot back to give the ball a firm kick, he was charged from behind and went crashing to the turf.

A whistle shrilled. Jabber turned to see the ref making the charging sign. Then he looked at his offender and wasn't surprised. It was Ace Merrill, the kid who had been on his tail most of the times that Jabber had the ball.

"Penalty kick!" called the ref.

Brushing off his legs and knees, Jabber spotted the ball on the penalty line and stepped back. The only player between him and the goal was the Razorback goalkeeper. All the others had to remain outside the penalty area, and at least ten yards from the ball.

Jabber picked his target, a spot near the left-hand corner of the net. Standing directly on the goal line, legs spread apart and arms ready to spring, was the black-shirted goalie.

Jabber started forward, running directly in line with the goalkeeper. Then — *thump!* Foot met ball, but at the very last instant Jabber aimed for a spot just to the right of center, and sent the ball streaking exactly where he wanted it to go.

The goalkeeper made a gallant effort, but in vain.

Jabber chalked up his second goal.

That was an accident. I'm sorry," said Ace.

"What?" asked Jabber of the aggressive Razorback player. "My scoring a goal?"

"No. My running into you. I didn't mean it."

Jabber shrugged. "That's okay. I'm not holding a grudge."

"Yeah. Well, I just wanted you to know," said Ace, and trotted off toward the center of the field.

"I heard that," said Mose, coming up beside Jabber. "If that was an accident, I'll eat my shorts. I saw him hit you, and I could tell it was no accident."

"I'm sure it wasn't either," said Jabber. "Oh, well — so what? Maybe he just got carried away at the time and won't do it again."

The Nuggets got possession of the ball after the center kick, moving it down close to the Razorbacks' penalty area before Ace himself got off an excellent kick that sent it back upfield. He bolted after it, Stork hot on his heels. In seconds all five defense-men — Mike, Jabber, Mose, Al, and Eddie — were in action, helping protect goalie Tommy Fitzpatrick from letting the ball go between the goalposts.

Ace Merrill was the toughest and the fastest of the Razorback bunch, and he proved it as he stayed as if glued to the ball.

Suddenly he passed it to a teammate, then rushed toward the goal. Catching a pass delivered to him, he quickly drilled it into the net past Tommy's flying body.

Nuggets 2, Razorbacks 1.

With three minutes to go before the half ended, an offside penalty on the part of the Razorbacks put the ball in the Nuggets' control. Seconds later the Nuggets maneuvered it into position for their third goal as Stork booted it in from eight yards out.

The score remained 3 to 1 in favor of the Nuggets when the half ended.

Jabber wished he could use part of the ten-minute intermission to talk to Pete, but Coach Pike wasted no time in heading for the wooded area just beyond the Nuggets' goal, and waving his charges to follow him just as soon as they got their jackets on.

The coach looked behind him and settled his gaze on his dark-haired, well-built center halfback.

"Nice going, Jabber," he said, patting the boy on his back. "You're playing soccer as if you've played it all your life."

"I haven't, though," said Jabber. "This is my first year."

"Yes, I know. And I'm glad you came out for the team. You're a natural, Jabber."

A natural? Pete had said the same thing to him. A natural what? Soccer player? Football player? Or did they simply mean a natural athlete?

Just before they reached the woods the coach stopped his players, and the kids sat on the grass while he talked to them. He was tough, bold, and blunt, and had a word for each of them.

"Joe," he said, pointing a finger at Joe Sanford, one of the backfield men, "did you skip lunch today? I saw you biting your nails like crazy. You're out there to get in and help defend that goal. And you, Butch. Don't slow down to a walk after you pass the ball. If you're tired, say so, and I'll put in somebody else. Eddie, use your head on some of those high bounces. I mean literally. We might have kept the ball in our control that one time when you stopped it with your chest, letting it bounce right at the feet of a Razorback. Okay?"

"Okay, Coach," Eddie Bailor responded.

On and on he went, finally directing a word of advice to Jabber. "Jabber, you're playing a nice game so far, but —" He held up a finger. "Don't be afraid to dribble with both feet. You're favoring your right, which is natural. But develop that left foot, too. Okay?"

"Okay."

The second half got under way. Seconds after the ball was centered a Razorback halfback booted it deep into Nugget territory. A teammate stopped it with his chest, then dribbled it a few yards before a trio of Nuggets converged on him. Jabber was one of them, and he tried to judge what the player would do when he realized he was going to be triple-teamed.

They were about ten yards from the goal line. As the trio rushed him, the player kicked. It might have been a long one, and it was aimed well toward the goal, but Jabber sprang in front of it. The ball deflected from his chest toward the touchline, bouncing out of bounds before one of his teammates could stop it.

"Green out!" yelled the ref.

A Razorback took it out, tossing the ball in with both hands. A teammate received the pass and gave it a hard boot toward the goal. Tommy caught it and heaved it back onto the field.

Joe Sanford received it, passed it to Rusty, and Rusty got off a volley kick that carried the ball close to the center line.

"Jabber!" called Stork, running up beside the half. "Head toward the sideline!"

Jabber did, running slowly, keeping his eyes on the ball. Mose had it, dribbling it diagonally across the field in the direction in which Jabber was heading.

Just as two Razorback players began to gang up on him, Mose passed to Stork. Stork moved it down a few yards, then gave the ball a hard boot toward the left corner. It landed in front of Jabber, who trapped it with his chest, then used his right knee to propel it toward the goal. Glancing up, he saw Stork bolting toward the goal area, no one near him.

Jabber kicked the ball. For an instant he was afraid he had kicked it too hard, for the ball was flying through the air at a shallow slant. But for Stork it seemed to be just right. Jumping up about a foot, he stopped the ball with his right foot, waited for it to drop, then kicked it violently.

The ball zipped across the ground into the right corner, and it was 4 to 1, Nuggets' favor.

Jabber ran up beside the tall center, and slapped him on the rump. "Nice play, Stork."

"That's what is called Stork strategy." The tall, easygoing center beamed. "We should try it again sometime."

They did, just seconds before the quarter ended. But this time it failed to work. The ball was intercepted by a Razorback defenseman and booted back up the field.

"Oh, well," said Stork disappointedly. "That's the way the ball bounces!"

The fourth quarter started off as if the Razorbacks had conserved most of their energy for this last period. Substitutes were in now, and seemed to play as well as the regulars. They were in control of the ball from the very start, advancing the ball closer and closer to the Nuggets' goal.

Jabber watched the threatening move from the sideline. It was the first time during the game that he wasn't playing. But he was thankful for the rest. He needed it. His legs had begun to ache. His lungs had been pumping like pistons. Good thing we have a 4-to-1 lead, he thought.

A minute and fifty seconds into the quarter Ace Merrill scored the Razorbacks' second goal. It had seemed inevitable for they had looked unstoppable in their drive.

After the ball was centered the threat loomed again. The Razorbacks' subs, fresh, loose, and full of energy, were moving the ball again deep into Nugget territory.

"Jabber, Rusty, Eddie," said Coach Pike as the ball went out-of-bounds, bringing an opportunity to send in substitutes. "Get in there. Hurry. And don't forget to report."

They reported to the scorekeeper, then rushed

out on the field, sending out the subs. It was the Nuggets' ball. Joe Sanford threw it in. Rusty got it, passed it to Eddie. Instantly two Razorbacks were upon him; they stole the ball from him as he fell, and dribbled it toward the Nuggets' goal.

A kick was aimed for the left corner, but this time Tommy was there for the save.

A pass and a long kick advanced the ball to the center line. Jabber sped toward it, trapped it between his knees, then kept it under control as he entered Razorback territory. He remembered the coach's advice about using both feet in dribbling, and tried to do it, but found it difficult. It wasn't easy to break from a habit that had become so comfortable for him.

Two Razorbacks charged at him. He feinted the ball away from one, then saw Stork close by and passed to him.

Stork took it and moved it toward the goal line, only to go sprawling on his stomach as a Razorback player rushed at him from behind.

A whistle shrilled. "Pushing!" yelled the ref. "Direct free-kick!"

15

Stork brushed himself off, kicked the ball from where it was spotted by the ref, and once more Jabber had it in his possession.

He got it into the penalty area and tried a long shallow kick. No good. The Razorbacks' goalie caught it.

Jabber and the whole Nuggets team were glad when the horn blew, announcing the end of the ball game.

Hey, you're good, man. You're really good."

"You mean it, Pete? You're not just saying that?"

"No, I mean it. You're really good. But you're in the wrong ball park."

Jabber stared at his brother. "Wrong? Oh, I know what you mean." He tried to force a laugh.

Pete was four inches taller than Jabber, broad around the shoulders, eyes dark, piercing. "I still can't see why you chose soccer over football, though, when you knew that Dad —" He hesitated, and shrugged.

"I know what you're going to say," said Jabber. "Yes, I know Dad played football in college. How can I forget it?"

"Well, he didn't just *play* football, Jabber," reminded Pete. "Dad became a star, and at Notre

Dame, too. That's something else, man. That's why I've gone out for football. Maybe I'll never be as good as Dad was, but you never can tell. With a great athlete like Dad as our father, we've got tremendous potential, you and I. And there's something else you should think about."

"What?"

"I think if Dad had lived he would have wanted you to play football."

"Maybe," said Jabber. Come on, Pete, will you? he thought.

"Maybe?" echoed Pete. "Heck, there's no maybe about it, Jab. You know yourself that's what he'd have loved to have you do. You sure surprised Mom too when you told her you were going out for soccer instead of football."

"I know."

Pete looked at him, frowning. "You know? And you still didn't change your mind?"

Jabber looked at the cracks in the sidewalk as he walked along. He wished that Pete would stop talking to him about Dad and football and soccer. It was bad enough to be reminded that his father had been killed in a freak car crash, and the football stuff just made it worse. He wished Pete would just shut up, or talk about something else. Hang-gliding, for instance. Pete liked that, too. He had taken it up in early spring and was doing pretty well at it. He would rather listen to Pete talk about that sport now than soccer or football. He hated to get mad at Pete. He had in the past, when they were much younger. But they were grown up now.

"Well," said Jabber, "I suppose I should tell you. I'm going to buy new soccer shoes."

Pete looked at him. "Oh? Whose have you been wearing?"

"One of the guys'. An old pair."

"I guess that clinches it then. Your playing soccer, I mean."

"Sort of," Jabber answered quietly.

They arrived home and found their mother and Karen setting the table for supper. Karen was seventeen, a senior at Birch Central, a budding poet, and senior editor of the school paper. She looked so much like her mother that they could pass for sisters.

"Well, I guess we've got this timed pretty well, haven't we?" said Mrs. Morris. "Who won?"

"We did," said Jabber, taking off his jacket. "Four to two."

"Do anything?" asked Karen. "Scorewise, I mean."

Jabber saw Pete heading into the next room, apparently uninterested in the conversation.

"I scored twice," said Jabber.

"Good!" exclaimed Karen cheerfully. "I wish I could've gone, but I had some layouts to take care of for our school paper. How was the crowd?"

Jabber shrugged. "So-so. A handful."

"A handful? That's all?" His mother stared at him, unbelieving.

"That's right. School soccer hasn't started to draw the people yet like football does. But it will. It just takes time."

"Was Pete at the game?" his mother asked.

"Yes."

"Oh. I thought he was going to go hang-gliding. Well, I'm glad he didn't go *there*."

Jabber knew that she wasn't crazy about Pete's love for hang-gliding. It was a dangerous sport, she contended, and he could easily break a leg, or suffer worse injuries.

She asked Jabber no further questions about the game, proceeding only to get the supper done and put on the table. The smell of roast beef and potatoes really stimulated Jabber's hunger, and he couldn't wait to get at them.

As his mother promised, supper was on the table in a minute. The four of them sat down and began their evening ritual. Jabber was first to finish, not realizing he had practically gulped it down until he glanced at the others' plates. Even Pete had a few spoonfuls left on his.

"Really were hungry, weren't you, brother?" Pete said, grinning. "Well, a lot of wild running and not getting anyplace will do that. Personally, it would drive me up a wall."

Jabber stared at him, then looked away, ignoring his brother's snide remark. Pete was implying that a player ran a lot more in soccer than he did in football.

So what? thought Jabber. What difference did it make? Each sport had its own characteristics, didn't it? But Jabber said nothing.

He noticed how quiet his mother had become. Now and again he looked at her, trying to catch her gaze, to read the thoughts behind her somber blue eyes. But she didn't give him a chance. He felt that she was holding back something from him, something that seemed to be bothering her.

It was when she was passing him the dish of beef for the second time that she broke her silence.

"Your Uncle Jerry called while you were gone," she said to Jabber. "He wanted to talk to you."

"Oh? He say about what?"

"Yes. He wants to take you to the Cornell-Colgate football game Saturday. He has a couple of tickets to it. He bought only two because he knows that Pete is playing Saturday too."

Jabber frowned, glanced at Pete, then back again at his mother.

"What lousy luck," he said. "I'm going to the high-school game, Mom. I'd like to see the Cornell-Colgate game, but I would rather watch Pete play."

"I told him I thought you would," she said.

"Darn! I hate to disappoint Uncle Jerry. He's always so good to us."

"Oh, I'm sure he won't mind. He had quite a time making a decision himself on which game to see.

But he had bought the tickets some time ago. He says that he'll try to sell them and go to the high-school game. I told him that he shouldn't. He can see Pete some other time."

Uncle Jerry was Mom's older brother. He and his wife Doris had no children. Jabber was certain that that was the reason the friendship between Uncle Jerry and his nephews and niece had become such a tight bond. He was a hardware store manager, and often stopped by with a supply of groceries for his sister's family.

"I know what your check is each week," he had said to her one day when she protested about his bringing the groceries. "Even with that insurance money you got from John's death, you've had tough sledding. Don't worry about me. Or Doris. She's with me every bit of the way. If we weren't able to help you out a little, we wouldn't. So don't worry about it. Okay?"

He was a big bear of a man, and as an ex–football player he took an avid interest in the athletic activities of his two nephews.

"Mom," Jabber said, "has Uncle Jerry said anything about my playing soccer?"

"Well — yes, he has."

"He doesn't like the idea, does he?"

She shrugged. "Well, figure it out for yourself. He played football. And your father played football."

"And Pete plays football," Karen added aggressively. "So what? Just because *they* played football does Jabber have to follow in their footsteps? Horseradish! He's got a mind of his own. He should do what he wants."

Jabber stared at her, startled. She usually didn't speak up on his behalf so boldly.

"Let's drop the subject," suggested Mrs. Morris. "The last thing I need is a headache over this silly discussion."

Karen looked at her, grim faced. "Silly? Mom, I know as well as you do that none of you like the idea of Jabber's playing soccer. I've heard you say at least two or three times that Daddy would have liked to see Jabber play football, too, if he were going into any sport at all. Now, didn't you say that?"

Mrs. Morris fixed her eyes on her daughter. She wasn't angry, but it wouldn't take much more for her to arrive at that point. "Yes, I said that, Karen," she said. "But you don't know everything, my dear daughter. Jerry told me that he'll help pay for part of Pete's college expenses, and also Javis's, but he would like to see Javis play football."

"And if 'Javis' doesn't play football?" Karen's eyes flashed. She hardly ever called Jabber by his actual name.

"He'll still help pay for it," answered Mrs. Morris. She appeared calm, but Jabber knew she was trying hard to hold back her emotions. "Your uncle is not inhuman, Karen. He cares for all of you. He just would be happier if Javis, like Pete, would follow in your father's footsteps. That's all."

"When did Uncle Jerry say he'd help pay for Pete's and my college expenses, Mom?" asked Jabber curiously.

"A few weeks ago. Maybe a month."

"And you said it was okay?"

"No. I said it wasn't okay. I told him there were scholarships available for children whose fathers were dead. But he said he'd help anyway. You should know your uncle. If he says he'll help pay, he'll help pay."

"He's the greatest," said Pete, smiling.

Jabber looked out the window. Dusk was falling fast. The forecast was for rain, and colder that night.

It was a miserable day, he thought. In more ways than one.

Birch Central won the game on Saturday, 28 to 24. Pete scored a touchdown on a thirty-four-yard run, and set up another one when he caught a sixteen-yard pass from his quarterback.

Uncle Jerry hadn't been able to sell his tickets to the Cornell-Colgate game, so he had gone to it alone. He called later, saying that Cornell had squeezed out a 15-to-14 victory over Colgate, and that Aunt Doris had caught a cold.

"At least that's what she said to me," Uncle Jerry said to Jabber over the telephone. "But she coughs so much from smoking so many cigarettes a day I don't know whether it's really a cold, or an excuse to stay home."

Jabber laughed. Uncle Jerry always said that his wife had two vices, one of which was smoking. He never said what the second one was, and Jabber suspected that keeping it a secret was just meant to tease Aunt Doris.

Jabber had a math test on Monday morning, and still had several problems to go when the period was over. Mrs. Williams gathered up his paper with the rest of the students' anyway.

"How do you think you did?" Mose asked him as they left the classroom.

"I think I flunked," said Jabber.

"Flunked? I thought it was a snap."

"You would. You're a genius."

"Oh, sure. One day I grab a ninety-two in a math test, and I'm a genius. If I had half your brain —"

"You'd be twice as dumb as I am," said Jabber.

In math class the next morning he found out that he had predicted correctly. He had flunked. His mark was a disappointing 63.

Mrs. Williams called him to her desk after class.

"That sixty-three mark seemed to be the work of another boy, not you, Javis," she said. She was one of the very few people — besides his mother — who called him by his actual name. "Didn't you study for the test? I warned you about it last Thursday."

"I studied for it," he said.

"But not enough, right?"

"Right," he answered.

"We're having another one Friday," she reminded him flatly. "It'll be a review of what we've learned during the last four weeks. I hope that you'll be able to bone up on it by then. Okay?"

"Okay."

He was glad that she didn't start asking him personal questions to determine why he had gotten such a low mark. He didn't know himself.

Liar, he thought. You know darn well why you didn't get a better mark than a crummy sixty-three.

The reason for it was soccer, and the hassle caused by his choice to play it instead of football. All the rest of his family, except Karen, thought he should play football because Dad had played in college. And Dad was dead.

An automobile crash took the lives of three community leaders last night as they headed for home from New York and got caught in the storm that hit them just south of Buffalo. Their car slid off the icy road and slammed head-on into a tree.

Only the driver, Edgar Mills of 213 Willow

Street, Birch Valley, survived. The others, John Morris, vice-president of Adams Electric . . .

His picture was above the newspaper article. A good-looking, broad-shouldered man. Tough, but kind. Firm, yet gentle.

He never told me he wanted me to play football, thought Jabber. Never.

Yet Mom and Pete made Jabber feel guilty because he didn't play football. Even Uncle Jerry's offer to help with college expenses, as good and kind as it was, made him feel guilty, too.

Darn it! Maybe I shouldn't play any sport at all! he thought disgustedly. Maybe I should just be a spectator!

He went to soccer practice after school. At the other field, which Jabber could see from the soccer field, the varsity football team was working out, too.

Coach Pike drilled them on one-on-one dribbling, then one-on-two, then on corner kicks. It was a cold day, and the wind was nippy. Only by running around was Jabber able to keep warm.

He got bone-tired after a while, and he didn't have a chance to rest. From then on he took it easy, moving fast only when he had to.

The football team finished before the soccer team did, and Pete stopped by and watched until the soccer team's practice was over. He didn't have to wait long. He and Jabber walked off the field and to the locker room together. They got out of their uniforms, showered, and dressed.

"I'm starved," Jabber said as they left the school. "I hope that Mom has some big juicy steaks for us. Or even hot dogs and sauerkraut."

"Don't bet on it," said Pete. "I think this is hamburger night."

"Yeah — well, I can go for them, too."

They walked for a while without saying anything. Jabber felt that Pete was deep in thought about something. Pete wasn't one to dwell in silence very long.

It came out finally.

"Funny thing happened today," he said. "Coach Pearce asked me about you."

"He did?" Jabber's eyebrows arched. "Why?"

"He heard you're playing soccer, and wondered why you didn't go out for football."

"Oh, man," said Jabber. "Everybody in this world is wondering why I didn't go out for football instead of soccer. What did you tell him?"

"Nothing. What could I tell him?" Pete was silent for a moment. "Anyway, I want to make sure you know what you're doing."

Jabber looked at him. He met Pete's eyes. They were serious. Sometimes he had seen his mother's eyes looking like that.

"Football is the game to get into, man," said Pete. "For us, anyway. You and me. Basketball is out, because neither one of us will ever get much over six feet tall. And we're just so-so in baseball. But in football we've got a chance. We've got a chance to play college football, then maybe go into the pros and clean up. There's money being tossed around like leaves for the football player who makes it big. Even if neither one of us becomes another Joe Montana or Emmitt Smith, we might still make extra bucks doing TV commercials, or endorsing shaving creams."

"Or deodorant."

"So what? It's still greenbacks. I don't know, Jabber. You must be out of your mind. You really must."

"I'm doing what I want to do," replied Jabber. "Do you know how few guys make the pros? Why do you think either one of us would make even one lousy commercial? I want to play for the fun of playing."

"But you've got to make a living sometime."

"I know. But I don't have to make it playing football."

"I don't believe it," said Pete, somewhat disgustedly. "You know that? I really don't believe it."

"Then let's not talk about it anymore."

"Okay. But one more thing," said Pete. "I see you haven't bought new soccer shoes yet."

"Not yet," said Jabber. "But I will soon."

"Wish you'd hold off," said Pete. Then he smiled and poked his brother gently on the shoulder. "Hey, man. How about coming with me to Knob Hill on Saturday?"

All at once there was a complete change in Jabber's attitude.

"Hang-gliding?" he asked.

"What else?" Pete grinned.

"Okay. I'll go with you," Jabber promised, happy that at last they had gotten off the subject of soccer versus football.

Jabber spent Wednesday and Thursday evenings studying for the math test on Friday. On the day of the test he sweated over the problems. It seemed that half of them were problems he hadn't studied about at all.

Now and then he looked up and saw Mrs. Williams's fierce blue eyes fastened on him. That made him more nervous than ever. He didn't know how he finished the test before the buzzer sounded, but he did.

"Wow!" said Mose as they left the room for their next class. "What a humdinger that was! I'll be lucky to get sixty!"

"I'll be lucky if she'll have me back in class," said Jabber.

Mose looked at him. "I'd be lucky if she *wouldn't* have me back in class!" he quipped.

Mose talked as if he didn't have a brain in his head. But he was an A student, racking up marks in the nineties most of the time. Playing soccer didn't seem to affect *his* studies a bit.

Pete was late coming home that afternoon. Maybe the football team was practicing, reflected Jabber. But that seemed unlikely. The team had never practiced on Fridays before.

Pete arrived home at last, an hour later than usual. The look on his face indicated that he was unhappy about something.

"Where have you been, Pete?" asked his mother. "It's almost suppertime."

"I lost my wallet and was searching for it," he answered, his jaw set with anger. "Tony Dranger and a couple of guys and I were playing touch football on the school grounds, and I must have lost it then. We all looked for it, but couldn't find it."

"Did you have any money in it?" asked Karen.

"Seventy-five bucks. Every dollar I had."

"Seventy-five bucks?" Karen echoed. "Why were you carrying that much money with you?"

"I was going to stop at Smitty's Sport Shop on the way home and buy me a pair of shoes. Football shoes."

Jabber stared at him.

Pete shrugged. "That's right, brother," he said. "After you mentioned that you were going to buy a pair of soccer shoes, I looked at my football shoes and figured I could stand a new pair myself. So — down the drain go the shoes, and somebody else is richer by seventy-five smackers."

"Was anybody around?" asked Karen.

"No one that I saw," Pete replied.

Jabber looked sympathetically at his brother. Seventy-five dollars, that wasn't hay. Now Pete would probably have to look for a part-time job to earn his money back.

They went to Knob Hill after lunch on Saturday with Tony Dranger. Tony, a senior at Birch Central, had a driver's license and a beat-up car that seated ten if it had to. They had two hang-gliders strapped to the roof.

Two other guys and two girls were already on the hill, flying hang-gliders in a wide sweeping turn over the valley below. The hill was steep, making it easy for takeoffs and flying. Jabber had already flown a few times, but not ascending higher than twenty feet or so. Pete and Tony were more experienced, having flown dozens of times and reaching altitudes of six hundred to seven hundred feet.

Tony parked the car in a lot below the hill. Then he and Pete removed the gliders from the roof and started to carry them up the steep incline.

"When are you going to get one of these wings?" Tony asked Jabber.

"I don't know," Jabber said.

"Like to fly 'em?"

Jabber shrugged. "It's fun," he admitted, not caring to elaborate.

They reached the top of the hill. Pete and Tony unfolded the wings and strapped on the harnesses. Pete's wing was yellow, Tony's red. The wind blowing up the hill made them flop up and down like huge anxious birds.

Tony took off first, running several steps down the incline before the wind caught the glider and lifted it into space. Pete followed him, sailing down toward the valley, then circling around, his feet dangling, like some prehistoric bird. Tony was flying as smoothly as an eagle, dipping down to pick up speed, then tipping up his wing for a gentle climb.

For a while he remained above Pete. Then Pete soared even higher, always in a circle, and Jabber could hear the boys yelling to each other. He felt an excitement just watching them, and wondered if someday he would be able to fly as expertly as they could. He had no immediate desire to do so, though. He preferred to be cautious, knowing that hang-gliding could be dangerous if you weren't careful every minute.

About fifteen minutes later Pete and Tony landed at the bottom of the hill, removed their wings, and walked back up.

"Want a go at it?" Pete asked Jabber as they reached the top.

Jabber thought a minute, then said, "Okay."

He strapped on the harness, grabbed the bar in front of him, then stood a moment gathering up his nerve.

"Go ahead," said Pete. "Just make sure you don't dip the nose too low or you'll ram into the ground."

Jabber nodded, remembering all he had learned

from his trial-and-error flights, then started running down the hill. Suddenly he felt the wind grab the sail in front, and he was off.

He thrilled at the feel of the wind blowing against him, the musical sound of it whistling past his ears, while the ground seemed to drop lower and lower beneath him. He held the front of the wing tipped down slightly to keep himself from rising too high, then circled above the valley, turning so that he could see his brother and Tony standing up there on the hill. They waved to him, and he could hear Pete shouting something.

A quick updraft lifted the nose of the wing, and Jabber almost panicked. Swiftly he brought the glider under control, and decided he had better call it quits.

Heart pounding, he started to head for the ground, and saw a car driving into the parking lot. He recognized it immediately as belonging to Uncle Jerry.

I wonder if he recognized me? Jabber thought, not sure whether his uncle knew that he had taken up the sport, too, as Pete had, and wondering if he'd approve when he found out.

He made a soft landing, took off the wing, and smiled nervously at Uncle Jerry, who had left his car and was coming toward him.

"Hi, Uncle Jerry!" he called.

"Hi, Jabber! Hey, you're doing all right, kid!" Apparently he didn't mind.

"Well, I'm getting better all the time," Jabber replied, the nervousness leaving him.

The tall man stepped up to him and shook his hand. "You had a hairy moment, though, didn't you?" he observed. "For a second I thought you were going to flip over when your wing tipped up."

Jabber nodded, remembering the frantic moment. "I handled it okay, though," he said.

"Yes, you did. I'll reassure your mom that you can take care of yourself on a wing."

They started up the hill, Jabber carrying the wing.

"Your mother said I'd find you guys here," said Uncle Jerry. "I had nothing to do so I thought I'd come over."

"I'm glad you did."

"How's your soccer team doing?"

"Okay."

"This your first year? I mean — you're a fresh-man, right?"

"No. I'm in the eighth grade."

"Oh. That's right." His uncle smiled. "I didn't think the middle school had a soccer team."

"Well, we do."

"I see." The tall man glanced up the hill and waved to Pete, who waved back. "Do you think you're going to continue playing soccer in high school, too, Jabber?"

"I don't know. I suppose so."

"Well —" His uncle cracked a broad smile. "Frankly, I'm surprised, Jabber. I thought you'd surely go for football, since your father had played it."

Jabber blushed. "I guess I've disappointed you, too, haven't I, Uncle Jerry?" he said.

His uncle put an arm around Jabber's shoulders and gave him a gentle squeeze. "Oh, I don't know. Soccer's come a long way. Maybe by the time you're in college — if you decide to go — soccer might be-come as popular as football. You never can tell."

"Well, Uncle Jerry," said Jabber seriously, "I don't

think I care if it becomes as popular as football or not. I just like to play it, that's all."

Uncle Jerry looked at him, his eyes narrowed soberly. "That's the *only* way to look at a sport, Jabber," he said.

They reached the top of the hill. Uncle Jerry shook Pete's hand, then Tony's. Pete asked him kiddingly if he was there to try his hand at hang-gliding.

"Not on your life!" exclaimed Uncle Jerry. "You go on and have your fun! I'll just watch!"

Jabber wondered, though, if his uncle's real reason for coming here was to watch them hang-glide, or to talk to him about his playing soccer.

At any rate, Uncle Jerry didn't push his point of view like Mom, or Pete.

6

That afternoon Jabber walked uptown and bought his soccer shoes. He felt funny about it, thinking that he was able to purchase his shoes, while Pete couldn't.

Well, it is pretty ridiculous to play touch football with a wallet in your pocket, reflected Jabber. Pete will just have to find some odd jobs and start saving his money again.

The shoes Jabber selected fit him perfectly. They were dark blue with three white slanting stripes on their sides, as neat looking as they were neat fitting. He received only a few cents in change from the bills he handed the clerk.

"Man, they're beauties," exclaimed Pete when Jabber arrived home and displayed his purchase to his family. "They must have set you back plenty."

"Not too bad," said Jabber, telling them the price.

"Wow!" groaned Karen. "For those?"

"Well," said Pete, shrugging his shoulders despairingly. "I guess I'll just have to wait awhile to get mine now."

"Oh, don't worry," said Mrs. Morris. "People are good-hearted. Someone will find your wallet and bring it back. Just wait and see."

"I'm waiting," replied Pete, cracking a wry smile that implied he didn't expect to ever see his wallet again.

The Nuggets tackled the Sabers on Tuesday afternoon. Jabber became a target for kidding the instant he put on his brand-new soccer shoes in the locker room.

"Oh, man! Look at them flashy shoes!"

"Hey, guys! Feast your eyes on that footwear!"

"Aren't you afraid you're going to get them all dirty, Jabber?"

He shrugged off the comments and rushed out on the field as quickly as he could. The ground was hard, the grass worn down in spots like an old rug. The sky was overcast and a strong wind blew, biting into Jabber's skin until he warmed up.

In a few minutes the field was alive with players from both teams, the Nuggets in their blue pants and gold shirts on the north side, the Sabers in their green pants and white shirts on the south side. Each team was kicking three or four balls. Now and then a player kicked a long shot, getting practice in case he might happen to draw a penalty shot or a free kick in the game.

Jabber stole a moment occasionally to size up the opponents. As was usually the case, some of them were tall, some short. Some of the short ones appeared faster and more aggressive than some of the tall ones, who seemed as if they were all legs and arms. Others were built like young bulls.

A few minutes before four o'clock, game time, Coach Pike's shrill whistle pulled his charges off the field. They huddled around him near the Nuggets' bench.

"Okay, men," he said, his shoulders hunched up against the wind. "These Sabers are as sharp as their name. They're fast. They're aggressive. They averaged four goals a game last year, and so far this year three. So get out there and show 'em. Show 'em you're not letting their record scare you. Show 'em you can make some of your own. Okay. Any questions?"

No one said a word.

"Okay. Fine. Be ready."

Jabber turned to look at the small crowd. He recognized Karen instantly, standing among some of her friends. She smiled, and waved. He waved back.

My best fan, he thought. Out of the whole family she's the only one who sticks up for me.

The game started. It was hardly a minute old before Jabber realized he had a tough customer playing opposite him. It was Nick Anders, one of the tall, big guys on the Sabers' team who could really move.

Nick stole the ball from him and dribbled it down the field about ten feet before giving it a long boot toward the goal.

"Hey, Jabber!" Jack Sylvan of the Nuggets yelled. "Afraid you'll get your shoes messed up?"

"Go fly a kite," murmured Jabber.

Jack laughed.

The Sabers' full front line — the wings, the forwards, and the center — was staging an aggressive attack to get the ball into the net. Nuggets Al Hogan and Eddie Bailor had their hands full as they tried to help goalie Tommy Fitzpatrick protect the goal.

A long kick by Nick Anders was stopped by Eddie, who tried to boot the ball toward the touchline and out of immediate danger. But another Saber flew in, trapped the ball with his chest, then hit it with his knee back toward the goal.

Jabber, running toward the center of the goal, saw Nick waiting near the edge of the net to accept the pass that would put him in excellent position to try for a score. Clenching his fists and drawing on all the stamina he could, Jabber changed direction and bolted toward Nick. He slipped and almost fell, but he regained his balance quickly and went on.

Just before the ball reached Nick, Jabber leaped in front of the Saber player and awkwardly struck the ball with his head. He felt the sudden shock all the way down to his knees, and for a moment saw an explosion of stars. As his vision cleared, he saw the blurred ball arching through the air up the field, and he ran after it.

A Saber started to converge upon it, and both he and Jabber reached it at the same time. They kicked it at the same time too, and the ball skittered off to the right, spinning madly.

While trying to twist around and get control of it, Jabber felt his opponent's legs get tangled with his. Both players lost their balance and fell. But Jabber was up almost as quickly as he had gone down, sprinting again after the ball.

He slowed down as he saw Mose stop the ball between his feet, then boot it up the field. Jack Sylvan caught the pass and moved it on, passing it to Butch Fleming. Butch dribbled it toward the Sabers' goal, only to lose it to a Saber defenseman who kicked the ball back up the field.

Now Mose was in front of it again, stopping it with his chest this time, then dribbling it.

Jabber, running up beside him, yelled, "Here, Mose!"

Mose passed it to him. Jabber dribbled it toward the goal, saw the open space to the goalie's left side, and aimed a hard shot toward it. His toe met the ball squarely, sending it booming like a cannon blast. The aim wasn't perfect, but it was good enough, as it just missed the top rod and rammed into the net.

Shouts exploded from the Nuggets' players and

fans. Jabber turned and began trotting back to his position at the other side of the field, hardly believing that he had punched a hole in the strong Sabers' defense. He felt that he had done the near impossible, and was both surprised and gratified at the same time.

He heard his name shouted from the fans standing along the sideline, and recognized Karen's high soprano voice.

"Nice shot, Jabber!"

"Good play, kid!" another fan yelled.

Could Karen really know how much scoring that goal meant to him? Perhaps. But what about his mother, and Pete, and Uncle Jerry, when they heard about it?

"You're wasting your energy in that sport" — that's what they'd say. "Football's the game you should be playing, not soccer."

Feet pounded on the turf beside him. A hand slapped him on the back. "Nice boot, Jab!" praised Mose Borman. "That's breaking the ol' camel's back!"

"Yeah!" said Jack Sylvan, coming up on Jabber's

other side. "But look what he did! Scuffed his brand-new shoes!"

Jabber grinned as he looked down at his dirt-smeared shoes. "I sure did, didn't I?" he said amiably.

The game resumed. The ball was placed back on the center of the field. The Sabers' tall center kicked. A teammate got it, booted it toward the left sideline. Jabber, seeing Butch hightailing for it in a race with the Sabers' left wing, headed toward the goal, ready to help the fullbacks and Tommy protect the net if need be.

The Saber got to the ball first, and kicked it farther down toward the end of the field. Eddie stopped it with his chest, let it drop to his feet, then started to kick it back up the field. As he did so, a Saber leaped in front of him and blocked the ball with his chest. Jabber saw the look of surprise spring into Eddie's eyes.

Jabber rushed toward the Saber and tried to steal the ball from him. Relentlessly they scrambled for it, Jabber knowing that the kid would be in excellent position for a goal kick if he weren't stopped soon.

Again and again Jabber looked for that split second when his opponent's feet wouldn't be in the way. The Saber seemed liked an octopus with all its tentacles writhing. He was an inch taller than Jabber, and slightly heavier. His legs were strong, bulging with muscles. Sweat shone on his arms. Jabber knew from the hard, deliberate way the kid was working the ball that he was determined to put it through the goal himself.

They were within ten yards of it now. Al and Eddie stood on each side of Tommy, assisting him in defending the wide vulnerable spots of the goal. Mike and Mose rushed at the Saber too, only to be blocked by other Sabers who acted as shields for their attacking wing.

Jabber felt an elbow jab his ribs. He didn't know whether it had been intentional or not, but no whistle shrilled.

Out of the corner of his eye Jabber could see the goal less than ten yards away. Even with Al, Eddie, and Tommy defending it, the spaces in between them looked like huge, inviting holes.

Suddenly the Saber cleverly drew the ball away from Jabber with the inside of his right foot, turned his back to block Jabber, then gave the ball a hefty kick with his left foot. Like a missile the ball boomed between Al and the side of the net. A goal!

Jabber turned away, gritting his teeth, as the Sabers' bench yelled their approval.

You should've got the ball off to me, Jab," said Mike Newburg critically. "I was clear a half a dozen times."

"I tried, but I couldn't," said Jabber. "That guy's tough. Who is he, anyway?"

"Mel Jones," said Mose. "Their left wing. He's their biggest scorer. We've got to watch him."

"Watch him?" echoed Jabber. "What'll that do? We've got to *stop* him."

He rubbed the cage of his ribs where Jones had hit him with an elbow. "He doesn't play too clean, either," Jabber added, still feeling the pain of that poke.

They were a minute into play again when the whistle blew, announcing the end of the first quarter.

The Nuggets' bench and their few faithful fans

tried to bolster the team's ego with a spirited cheer led by their cheerleaders, but Jabber hardly heard the chant. He felt responsible for the Sabers' score. During one of those moments when he and the Saber were struggling for control of the ball, he should have kicked it away.

"I was dumb," he blamed himself silently. "I could have kicked it away. I know I could have."

He was glad Pete wasn't present to have seen the play. Pete would have made some kind of cynical remark about it.

A few minutes after play resumed the Nuggets had the ball deep along the right sideline in Saber territory. Then a brief scramble for its possession resulted in its sailing out-of-bounds.

"White!" yelled the ref.

The Sabers took the ball, tossing it inbounds. Two hefty kicks got it into Nugget territory, and once again Jabber saw Mel Jones sprinting after it. The ball hit the ground, bounced up high, and seemed to take an eternity coming back to earth. But when it did Mel Jones and Jabber were there waiting for it.

As if both had the same idea, they leaped for the

ball, intending to strike it with their heads. Instead, they collided. Neither one touched the ball; it dropped behind them.

As the two players came down side by side, Jabber felt Mel Jones's elbow jab him in the ribs again. This time it hit deeper, feeling like a pointed ramrod as it knocked him off balance. He dropped to his side on the ground, his anger flaring.

A whistle shrilled, and Jabber heard the ref yell, "Elbowing! Direct free-kick!"

But the words bounced off Jabber's ears as he scrambled to his feet, his hands balled into fists. Rushing at the Saber player, he grabbed him by a shoulder and spun him around.

"Jones!" he snapped, his eyes flashing fire. "That's the second time you've done that!"

Mel Jones stared innocently at him. "Done what?" he snarled.

"Elbowed me!"

The whistle shrilled again. "Okay, you guys! Cut it out unless you both want to get kicked out of the game!" warned the ref.

A crooked grin crossed Mel's face. "You hear that, Morris?"

"Yes, I hear that," replied Jabber, his anger simmering. "But don't you elbow me like that again." He walked briskly away.

"Here," said the ref, handing Jabber the ball. "Take your shot from where the foul happened."

Jabber placed the ball on the ground and stepped back, lining it up with the Sabers' goal.

"Give it a long shot, Jab!" Stork yelled.

Stork, all six-feet-three of him, was standing just beyond the center line, his long arms dangling at his sides. To his left were Jack Sylvan and Joe Sanford. Joe, a wing, was playing close to the touchline.

Jabber ran up to the ball and booted it. Instead of aiming it for Stork, however, he met the ball slightly on its right side and kicked it over the center line toward Joe. The ball, spinning counterclockwise, curved through the air and came down neatly in front of the wing.

At the same time, half a dozen Sabers rushed for the ball like a flock of birds after food. Jabber was moving too, rushing up the center behind Stork, who now had started to run toward the Sabers' goal.

Joe, stopping the spinning ball with his right foot, kicked it down the field closer to the goal line. It seemed like an aimless kick, and some of the guys let him know it.

"Hey, Joe! Who's down there?"

"Wrong direction, buddy!"

Jabber couldn't help letting a soft smile cross his face. The guys were forgetting that they often committed foolish mistakes themselves. You weren't always able to think reasonably under pressure. And Joe had been under a lot of pressure during those few precious moments before he had kicked the ball.

The ball bounced out-of-bounds. "White!" shouted the ref.

A Saber got the ball, stood behind the touchline with the ball over his head, and tossed it back onto the field to a teammate. The teammate stopped it with his chest and booted it up the field toward Nugget territory.

Stork and two Sabers raced after it, Stork's long legs rising and falling in a blur. He reached the ball first, kicking it softly at an angle back up the field. Jack got it and dribbled it a couple of yards before a Saber rushed at him. Jabber recognized the strong-muscled body immediately. It was Mel Jones.

Somehow Jack managed to kick the ball away

from Mel, and it skittered freely across the open space. Jabber and Mike, the closest to the play, sprinted after it.

Suddenly Mike, who was losing the race to Jabber, ran off to the side. "To your right, Jab!" he yelled.

Jabber got the message, but he had to get control of the ball first. And Mel was no easy man to contend with.

They both arrived at the ball simultaneously. Their right feet met the ball simultaneously too, resulting in a crunching sound that did nothing to the ball except almost rivet it to the ground.

Again and again they kicked the ball — abusing it, roughing it up — both staying in front of it to keep it from zipping by.

Jabber felt sharp dull pains each time the ball struck his ankles or shins, but he knew that Mel was feeling his blows, too. Jabber was tiring, and could feel the sweat drenching his face.

Then Mel got the kick that freed the ball. Pursuing it, his leg struck Jabber's, knocking Jabber off balance. Dismayed at having lost that brief battle, Jabber watched the Saber dribble the ball away and then kick it toward the Nuggets' goal.

Mel glanced back at Jabber, a wry smile coming over his face, as if to tease his opponent. Mel Jones had beat him again, Jabber realized. A cool cat, that Mel. But he could afford to be. He had the size, and he knew it.

Jabber got his breath back and started to run down the field, just as the buzzer sounded from the bench, announcing the end of the first half.

"Good going, men," Coach Pike praised his charges as he led them across the field. "One and one is a darn good score against those kids. You're playing A-one ball."

Mose, walking alongside Jabber, jackets over their shoulders, glanced down at Jabber's shoes. "Oh, man, look at those new shoes! You sure initiated them!"

Jabber shook his head mournfully. "I ought to send Jones a bill. He's responsible for all that dirt."

Mose grinned. "He's really giving you a hard time, isn't he?"

"Well — something like that," admitted Jabber, remembering the close battles he had with Jones while trying to get control of the ball.

"He made you mad out there too, didn't he, Jab?" said Jack, his sweaty face grinning.

"Mad? Well, yes, he did," said Jabber, feeling slightly embarrassed that Jack had brought it up. He hated losing his temper, considering it childish and beneath his dignity.

"He stole the ball away from you twice," continued Jack.

"The guy's bigger than Jabber," Mose said, defending his friend. "Anyway, Jabber gave him a battle. Jones knew that he wasn't up against just *anybody.*"

Jack laughed. "Yeah, I know," he said, and walked away.

Mose nudged Jabber on the arm. "There's one in every crowd," he said.

Jabber, forcing a grin to hide his feelings, said nothing.

The team paused on a sloping ridge some fifteen yards beyond the goal line, pulled their jackets snugly about their shoulders and necks, and sat down on the grass.

The coach looked at Jabber. "You and the Jones

kid really had it hot and heavy out there, didn't you?" he said amusedly.

Jabber shrugged. "He's aggressive, and I try to be," he answered calmly.

"You're doing all right, Jabber," replied the coach. "We need better passing, though. I know it's easier said than done, but against the Sabers we've got to work at it harder. Use the long kicks only when we're defending our goal. In their territory try to keep the kicks short. Use your heads." He chuckled drily. "Literally."

The second half got under way with some substitutions made. Pat O'Donnell replaced Mose at right half, Nick Franko replaced Eddie at right fullback, and Jerry Bunning replaced Joe Sanford at left wing.

Jabber wondered if the coach was wise to take Mose out. In Jabber's opinion Mose was the best half of the lot. But he knew he was prejudiced. Mose was his best friend.

Fifty seconds into the second half Butch booted the ball from the touchline to Jabber, who was in open country, not a player within ten yards of him. Jabber trapped the ball with his legs, and began dribbling it upfield, when two Sabers charged him. Neither one was Jones. Nor was either one as big as Jones. But both seemed equally aggressive.

They went after the ball as if he weren't even there. But the agility in their moves when they reached him proved that they were aware of him all right. Both started to kick the ball at the same time, as if they played on opposite teams. The move surprised Jabber, and he didn't know what to think of it.

Without wasting another second to try to figure it out, he kicked the ball hard up the field, where it glanced off the thigh of a Saber. He bolted after it, a sinking feeling coming over him as he saw that the ball was flying directly at another Saber. It was another one of those thoughtless, way-off shots, he reflected dismally.

The Saber stopped it with his chest and deflected it back down the field, a gentle tap that put it into position for another Saber. This second player was Nick Anders, that tough center half. Without waiting for the ball to slow down, Nick charged it and gave it a vicious boot.

It was an angle shot, heading for the right side corner of the Nuggets' goal.

"Get it, Tommy! Get it!" yelled the Nuggets.

Tommy sprang after it, leaping out almost horizontally after the ball at the last instant.

He missed it, and the kick scored.

Sabers 2, Nuggets 1.

"They double-teamed you, Jabber," said Mike, as they returned to their positions.

"They sure did something," admitted Jabber, wiping the sweat off his forehead.

There was a lot of running and passing during the rest of the quarter, but no goals.

Two minutes into the fourth quarter Jabber saw the field open before him. They were in Saber territory, and Stork had possession of the ball. He was dribbling it up the field, cleverly keeping it away from his defenseman with short, gentle pushes of his feet.

Look at me! Look at me! Jabber wanted to yell.

Suddenly Stork kicked the ball, a perfect pass directly to Jabber! Jabber almost grinned as he stopped the pass with his right leg and jockeyed it into position for a kick.

At once he saw two Sabers converging upon him, the same two who had charged him before. Perhaps

Mike was right. Perhaps he was being purposely double-teamed.

Glancing out of the corner of his eye he spotted Butch down near the right side of the Sabers' goal. Quickly he kicked the ball, a gentle tap that sent it across the ground in a direct line toward Butch.

Butch stopped it. Without missing a step he positioned the ball and booted it.

Smack into the net!

"Nice move, Butch!" yelled Pat, jumping on him happily.

Butch grinned as he looked with a surprised expression at Jabber. "Hey, man! I never expected that!"

"You've got to keep your eyes open every minute in this game," said Jabber happily.

"Well, it's two up," reminded Stork. "At least we're proving that we're an even match with those guys. They're not shellacking us as they had expected to do."

As the game deepened into its final quarter, Jabber could see a change in the players. None was running as much as he had during the early quarters.

Each player was tired, feeling the aches and pains in every part of his body.

I'm getting tired, he thought. But I'd hate to leave here without winning. They're a cocky bunch. We've *got* to win.

Two and a half minutes to go. Mel Jones had the ball in control deep in Nugget territory, dribbling it rapidly toward the goal with short, accurate taps.

Al and Nick converged on him. Quickly, as if he had expected the move from them, Mel kicked it to the right. Nick Anders was there, waiting for it.

But so was Jabber. He had anticipated the strategy when he saw Nick running to the spot and stopping there.

Running as fast as he could, Jabber intercepted the ball, booted it back up the field, and pursued it into Saber territory.

He saw Jerry running toward the left side of the goal and kicked the ball to him.

"Back to me, Jerry!" he yelled.

Jerry kicked the ball back to Jabber. But now the

Sabers' two fullbacks were ganging up on him, and he was feeling more tired than ever before. Sharp pains in his calves felt like needles. Sweat was dripping into his eyes, and the ball was a big round blur before him.

The two fullbacks were almost upon him now. He could hear their stomping feet, could almost hear their breathing.

Quickly he kicked the ball, aiming it between the goalie and the right post.

The ball missed his aim by over a foot. It zoomed toward the goalie, who had only to leap a few feet to catch it.

"Oh, no!" Jabber moaned.

The Saber players yelled their approval of their goalkeeper's easy save. One guy jumped on him and hugged him. The play had saved the game from going to the Nuggets.

It was the Sabers' ball as it was put back into play. They got it moving quickly into Nugget territory, Mel Jones's clever footwork being mostly responsible. Jabber didn't think he had ever seen anyone as clever at dribbling the ball as Mel.

Jabber ran down the field — slowly — to catch his breath, to get back some strength into his legs. He had given the play near the goal all he had. He had been sure he'd had it made.

Darn! he thought. What lousy luck! The game was going to be over in a few minutes. That score would have clinched it for the Nuggets.

He picked up speed and ran across the center line as he saw Stork boot the ball away from Mel. There was a mad scramble for it as Jerry Bunning, Mike Newburg, and a Saber converged on it. The Sabers' player got to it first, and gave the ball a vicious, arching kick down toward the Nuggets' goal line. Another Saber got under it, met it squarely with his head, and sent it bouncing toward the corner of the net.

Maybe he had planned it that way. Maybe he hadn't. Anyway, a Saber got to the ball and kicked it hard into the net. Tommy Fitzpatrick's dive gave him nothing but a dirt-smeared belly.

Sabers 3, Nuggets 2.

A yell of excitement sprang from the Sabers' followers, a scream of frustration from the handful of Nuggets' fans.

Jabber turned and drove the toe of his right shoe angrily into the turf. How do you like that? A goal on a freak play like that! No wonder those Sabers have been winning. They play by luck!

Oh, well. Of course that wasn't so. No team won on luck alone. The Sabers were good. You couldn't take that away from them. They had worked for those points. They just have more going for them this time than we do, reflected Jabber as he headed disappointedly back to his half position.

The game was over in another thirty-five seconds, ending with a yell from the Sabers, who jumped and hugged each other, and then ran to each of the Nuggets' players and shook hands.

"Nice game, Jabber," said Mel Jones, obviously the Sabers' star athlete.

Jabber grinned. "Thanks, Mel. You too."

After taking his shower he walked home with Mose, talking about the errors that resulted in their losing the game, and the "ifs" that might have helped them win it. The pair split up two blocks away from Jabber's home.

Tired, and deep in thought, Jabber almost missed

seeing the black leather object lying near the bush a few feet away from the sidewalk. Frowning, he stared at it a moment before going over and picking it up.

It was a wallet.

9

It was black and made of leather.

It looked worn. Jabber felt that he had seen that wallet before, but he wasn't sure.

He opened it. His first glance was at the white identification card in the front of it. His heart sang as he read the printed name: Peter Morris.

It *was* Pete's!

He opened the section that held the bills. His heart quit singing.

It was empty.

His fingers trembled as he searched for a secret compartment. Some wallets had them. But this one didn't. It had no bills in it. No coins. It had been cleaned out completely.

He started for the house a short distance away, anxious to tell Pete that he had found his wallet.

After a dozen hasty paces he slowed down. The frown reemerged on his forehead. His nervousness increased.

Wouldn't Pete wonder what a coincidence it was that he, Jabber, had found the wallet and not someone else?

And he'd want to know the answer to the sixty-four-dollar question, too: Where was the money that had been in it? The seventy-five dollars?

Ask the guy who had found the wallet in the first place, the guy who had tossed it near the bush, Jabber would say.

Oh, yeah? Well, who is the guy? Pete might say. How do I know that it wasn't you who found it in the first place? How do I know it wasn't you who stole the money from it? You think I forgot about the time a few years ago when you stole a couple of dollars from me? Sure you said you needed it and intended to pay me back. But how would I know that if I had not found out you had stolen it?

You bought a pair of soccer shoes, now didn't you? Shoes that set you back a good sum of money. How do I know that you're not the culprit? If you stole from me before you just might steal from me again.

Oh, man! What a pickle! thought Jabber. What should I do? If I tell Pete the truth, how can I be sure he'll believe me?

Jabber stuck the wallet into his pocket and walked to the house, taking the narrow sidewalk around the side to the back. He wished now that Karen had waited for him and walked home with him. It would've been so simple then. Either one could have found the wallet, and the other would have been a witness to it.

The way it had happened, he had no witness. There could have been money in it, or there could not have been. Pete could only take Jabber's word for it.

I should have tossed it back into the bush, he told himself.

"Speak about the devil," Karen said as he entered the kitchen. "What took you so long?"

"I showered," he said. "Don't I always shower?"

"Yes. But it just seemed you took longer than usual." Karen shook her head. "What a game to lose. I was telling Mom and Pete about it. Too bad that kick of yours missed. That would have won the game."

"I keep telling her it would still have been a tie," said Pete. He was at the table where his mother was beginning to place the dishes. "If the Sabers had scored a goal, that would have made it three and three, wouldn't it? It doesn't take a genius to figure that out."

Jabber shrugged. He had difficulty meeting Pete's eyes. *How good is Pete at reading faces? Can he tell that something is seriously bothering me?*

"You look as if you left your heart at the field," said his mother. "I remember that same look on your father's face when he'd come home after a loss."

"Soccer isn't any different, Mom," said Jabber.

He went to the sink and poured himself a glass of water.

"Karen said you played like a star," his mother went on. "When your father played football like that the whole town would hear about it. The whole town? Hah! The whole country!"

"That was when he was playing in college and in the pros, Mom," said Jabber. "The whole country doesn't hear about a kid playing on a junior high school team."

He swallowed the drink, placed the glass on the counter, and sat down at the table.

"But the town would hear about your playing if that was a football game," said Pete. "Look at me. I'm no star — not that I'm not working at it — but even so, everybody who reads the sports pages in Birch Valley knows who Pete Morris is. They even recognize me on the street. 'Hi, Pete,' they say. 'Good game you played.' It's a good feeling, I tell you."

"Of course it's a good feeling," said Mrs. Morris. "But don't say you're no star, Peter. You're the best Birch Central's got. You're like your father when he was your age."

Pete laughed. "You're just prejudiced, Mom. But don't stop saying that. I like to hear it."

"Sure you like to hear it," Karen intervened caustically. "Anything that feeds your ego."

"Of course I'm proud when I play well, if that's what you're saying," said Pete, his voice rising as he glared at his sister. "You don't belong in this conversation, anyway. You don't play any sports. What do you know about it?"

"According to your definition, football must be

the only sport," she exclaimed, her eyes flashing. "I play volleyball. But how would you know? You've never come to watch *me* play."

"Okay, okay. I'm sorry. I forgot you play volleyball." Pete lowered his head and ran his fingers through his thick black hair. "Anyway, that doesn't change the complexion of things. I still think that Jabber owes it to Dad's memory to be a football player."

"And *I* don't think he does," said Karen.

"You may not understand Pete's feelings, Karen," said Mrs. Morris. "You're seventeen years old, and you're a smart girl, I'm not taking that away from you. In fact, I'm very proud of you. But at seventeen you've still got a lot to learn. I'm in my forties, and Lord knows I've still got a lot to learn too."

"I'm glad you said that, Mom," Karen said, smiling.

"Your father loved football very much," Mrs. Morris went on. "He played it when he was a young boy. He played it when he was in high school. How do you think he was able to go to college? It was on a football scholarship. He never paid a penny for his college education. Then he played professionally, and made a lot of money. We didn't get rich, but we lived quite comfortably. Almost too comfortably, because we didn't save much money. Even when he retired and went into business your father didn't believe in having a lot of money stuck away in the savings bank." She chuckled drily. "I should talk. I guess I didn't, either. Anyway, that all ended when he got killed in the accident."

She paused briefly. She was having a hard time keeping her emotions under control.

"When you boys were born he bought a football and a helmet for each of you," she went on. "The footballs have long since worn out, but the helmets still hang in your closets. That was indication enough that he wanted both of you to play the one sport he liked best. And Jabber, though you can do what you want, remember that sport wasn't soccer."

It hurt Jabber to listen to her reminding him about it. She had hinted at it before, but this was the first time she had really laid it on the line.

Well, of course, much of what she and Pete said was true. Football was a great sport. And maybe if his father had played soccer, Mom and Pete would have felt the same way about it. But maybe they didn't understand everything, either. How could they? Neither one of them could possibly understand *everything*.

"One thing you two don't seem to understand," Jabber addressed his mother and Pete, "is that I enjoy soccer, and I don't enjoy football. And if you don't enjoy a sport, how could you be good at it?"

"I can't see any red-blooded kid not enjoying football," Pete said.

"Oh, come off that," Karen broke in. "You can't be serious."

"Serious? Listen —"

"Okay, okay." Mrs. Morris interrupted Pete as she and Karen placed the pots of steaming chicken, potatoes, and baby lima beans on the table. "Let's quit talking about football and soccer before the subject really gets out of hand. Anyway, I'm starving."

Jabber sat down, glad that the soccer-football controversy was over for the moment, and suddenly felt the lump in his back pocket. The lump that was Pete's wallet.

His decision whether to tell Pete about it or not swung back and forth like a pendulum. Should he or should he not take it out and hand it over to Pete? And what would Pete say?

"Jabber, did you hear me?"

He looked at his mother. "I'm sorry, Mom. What did you say?"

"Hold your dish up here so that I can give you some potatoes," she said. "Where's your mind, anyway? On the moon?"

His hand wasn't too steady as he held up the dish.

"You're awfully nervous," his mother observed. "Did our talk cause it? I'm sorry."

"When are you going to make hot dogs and sauerkraut again?" he asked. "You haven't made it in a long time."

"One of these days," she said.

"Hot dogs and sauerkraut," mimicked Karen. "Blah!"

Jabber put the dish down. His mother served the others and they began to eat. Not another word was said about sports. Most of the conversation was dominated by Mrs. Morris, who seemed to have a lot to tell about the people she worked with at the office.

Jabber paid very little attention to her. He didn't

know any of the people she was talking about. And tonight he couldn't seem to get interested in them.

It was the lump in his back pocket that he was concerned about. How long was he going to keep it there before he'd tell Pete about it?

Maybe they were right. Maybe he should quit soccer and shift to football.

He thought about it as he lay on his back in his room later that evening. It was a small room, containing just his single bed, a small desk, and two long shelves under the wide windows. The shelves were filled with books and magazines his parents had started to subscribe to for him when he was seven years old. One of the magazines, *Nature Life,* still came.

He thought about the rugged game he had played that day. Practically knocked himself out running up and down the field. And being bushed when he had attempted that goal.

Pete was right. You do an awful lot of running in soccer.

But you also run a lot in football. If it wasn't running, it was guarding, or tackling. But it wasn't as fast a game as soccer.

When you boys were born he bought a football and a helmet for each of you: his mother's words rang again through his mind. *That was indication enough that he wanted both of you to play the one sport he liked best. And Jabber, though you can do what you want, remember that sport wasn't soccer.*

He had loved his father. John Morris was a strong-willed man who didn't smoke or drink. He had laid down a law in the house that he expected to be obeyed. But he was also as warm and gentle as he was strict. He took the kids to circuses, carnivals, rodeos, and sports events. He bought them candy, ice cream, hot dogs, and hamburgers. What he didn't do was give them money freely. He didn't believe in that. "You'll learn the value of money when you get older and have to work for it," he had said.

Restless, Jabber turned and lay for a while on his stomach. Pete and his mother had made him feel guilty. *If you don't play football you don't love your father.* That was what they were telling him.

They were so wrong. He loved his father as much as they did.

He just didn't care for football.

He took the wallet out of his pocket and looked at it again. It was like some vial of poison in his hand. He wished he had never seen it, never picked it up.

The Nuggets played the Blue Jackets on Thursday afternoon, a game Jabber wasn't looking forward to. He had too much on his mind to enjoy playing soccer. The guilty feeling about not playing football — and Pete's wallet.

The Blue Jackets scored a goal just before the first quarter ended. But it was on a penalty shot. Jack Sylvan had been accused of tripping one of the Blue Jackets' players.

In general, the Blue Jackets looked only half as good as the Sabers. They lacked finesse. They had no big men. They should have been knocked off easily.

But Jabber wasn't playing as he had in the Sabers game. As if he didn't know it himself, Coach Pike had to rub it in. "What's the matter, Jabber? You have weights on your legs? You're not running like the old Jab."

"Maybe it's his shoes, Coach," Stork Pickering gibed. "Look at 'em. They're all cleaned up. Maybe he doesn't want to get them dirty again."

"Very funny, Stork," snorted Jabber.

Jabber tried to improve his performance, but his heart wasn't in it. He was glad when Mike kicked a goal in the middle of the second quarter to tie up the score.

The coach took Jabber out with four minutes to go in the half.

"You look tired, Jab," he said. "Or maybe you're not feeling well. Don't hold back on me. I don't want a kid playing if he isn't up to par."

"I'm telling you the truth, Coach," said Jabber. "I'm okay."

"Then why aren't you showing it on the field?"

"I'll try better the next half," Jabber promised. "If I'm in there," he added hopefully.

The coach made no comment about putting Jabber in or not, leaving Jabber wondering about it during the rest of the half, and the first few minutes of the ten-minute intermission.

Then the coach looked at him over the heads of the other players. "Okay, Jabber. You're starting the second half. Work close with Stork and Mose. Keep your kicks short, and let's break the game wide open. You ready?" he addressed the team.

"Ready!" they shouted in unison.

The buzzer sounded from the scorekeeper's bench, and both teams trotted onto the field. The starting lineup for each team got into position; the others sauntered over to their respective benches.

It was the Nuggets' turn to center the ball. Stork kicked it gently at an angle toward Rusty. The Blue Jackets' center tore in quickly, kicked the ball hard down the field, then led his team in a mad dash after it.

Eddie Bailor trapped the ball with his chest, and booted it back up the field. Eddie had strong legs and it seemed he could kick the ball a mile. He sent it almost to the center line where Rusty was waiting for it.

Jabber and Stork raced past Rusty, one on each side of him. Rusty passed it to Stork, who almost lost it the very next instant as a Blue Jacket came charging at him.

"Here, Stork!" cried Jabber.

Stork snapped the ball to him with the side of his foot, and Jabber took it down the field. He looked for Mose and saw the right half about ten feet away from him, to his right. Mose was okay. He was on the alert.

Two Blue Jackets converged on Jabber. He waited till the last moment he felt he could contain the ball, then shot it to Mose. Mose caught it expertly with the instep of his right foot and dribbled it on.

The two Blue Jackets turned and raced after the ball, one tripping over a leg of the other, falling to the turf and skidding a couple of feet.

Jabber leaped over him, heading down the center of the field. Ahead and to his right was Stork. Rusty and Butch were just beyond.

A Blue Jacket fullback charged at the ball, forcing Mose to kick. He intended it for Stork, but a Blue Jacket rushed in like a blur and kicked it, lofting it over the goal line.

"Gold out!" yelled the ref.

Jabber shook his head. A goal play had been in the making. If the ball had gotten to Stork, he would have passed it to Jabber and that would have been it. But the darn Blue Jacket had spoiled it.

Rusty took out the ball. He tossed it to Butch, who booted it gently *upfield* from the goal.

Jabber stared at him. "Butch! I was wide open!"

"You couldn't have scored, though," answered Butch. "You would've been offside."

Glancing quickly around him, Jabber saw that Butch was right. There would have been only one opponent between him and the goal line. The rules called for two.

"Sorry, Butch," he said, looking back toward the play in time to see Stork give the ball a vicious kick. It was a solid drive that streaked between two Blue Jackets like a cannonball toward the left side of the goal.

The Blue Jackets' goalie leaped after it, but not even a flying tackle could have stopped that one.

Nuggets 2, Blue Jackets 1.

Jabber headed slowly toward his position, feeling better now that the tie had been broken. He wiped the sweat off his forehead and his eyelids. His tongue felt like sandpaper. His throat was parched.

A kid ran onto the field with a bucket of water.

Each player took a few sips. Jabber took a swallow, swished some of the water around in his mouth and spat it out. He felt better.

During the free moment he couldn't help thinking again about Pete's wallet. He had to do something. He couldn't carry it around in his pocket forever.

If only somebody would break into his locker and steal it. But that would be asking for a miracle.

"Hey, Jabber," said Mose, interrupting his thoughts. "Where's your mind, man?"

Jabber pointed to his head. "Here."

"Are you sure? I called you twice."

"Maybe I'm getting deaf," said Jabber.

"I'll let you borrow my grandfather's hearing aid," Mose kidded him. "Maybe I'll sell it to you. He hardly ever wears it, anyway."

"I'll think about it," said Jabber.

Mose frowned at him. "Are you sure you're okay, Jab? I feel like the coach does. I think that you're either not well, or something's burning a hole in your head."

Jabber grinned. "You a psychiatrist or something?"

"No. But I can see that something's bothering you. I'm not that dumb. And if I can see it, you can bet Coach Pike can see it, too."

"What would you say," said Jabber suddenly, "if I quit soccer and played football?"

Mose's eyes widened. "You've blown your mind, that's what I'd say. You're not serious, I hope?"

"I don't know if I am or not. All I know is that my mother, my brother Pete, and my Uncle Jerry all want me to play football."

A whistle shrilled. "Let's go! Let's go!" yelled the ref.

"I'd think a lot about it if I were you!" cried Mose as they scampered to their positions.

The Nuggets threatened again to score, getting down close enough to the goal line to keep the Blue Jackets' goalie crouched and waiting. Stork stopped a pass from Rusty with his chest and kicked the ball to Jabber, who was running toward the goal area, in excellent position for a goal attempt.

A Blue Jacket fullback came rushing at Jabber, trying to meet the ball before it reached him. Taking a quick couple of steps forward to kick the ball before the player was upon him, Jabber lost some of his timing, and his aim was off. The ball careened off to the left, struck the oncoming player, and rico-cheted back up the field.

"Nuts!" grumbled Jabber, gritting his teeth as he spun after the ball.

Mike Newburg kicked it back, only to bounce it against another Blue Jacket player. The ball, hitting the player in the stomach, stopped his forward progress for a moment and bounced back in the di-rection of the Nuggets' goal.

Jabber thought that the blow might have knocked the wind out of the kid, but it didn't. The player, short and stout as a tree trunk, was back in action af-ter very little delay.

He kicked the ball far upfield, then pursued it like a hungry lion. Al Hogan kicked it back, lofting it high into the air, and gaining half a dozen yards on the exchange. The kick gave Jabber and Mose time to get under the ball, and to pass it back and forth until they had it again in Blue Jacket territory.

Jabber wasn't pleased with himself. He should have had a goal on that play a while ago. He would have, if he hadn't lost his timing and muffed it.

The buzzer sounded. It was the end of the third quarter.

"Take a rest for a while," said Coach Pike to Jabber, after Pat O'Donnell had run in to substitute for the halfback. "You were running pretty hard out there. As a matter of fact, you seemed to be overdoing it. You sure nothing's wrong with you?"

"I'm just a little bushed," said Jabber, breathing hard and wiping his sweating face with a towel.

"I can see that," replied the coach. "What I can't see is what is in that brain of yours. I know something's bothering you. Did you rob a bank? Or did you buy a car and discover you can't make the payments?"

Jabber laughed.

The coach patted him on the shoulder. "Okay. Don't tell me. If it's a family problem, I probably don't want to hear it, anyway. Sit down and put on a jacket. I don't want you to be catching pneumonia on top of whatever else is bothering you."

Jabber sat on the bench for almost six minutes of the final quarter. He didn't care much if he went into the game again or not. He hadn't been psyched up about it before it had started, and he certainly wasn't now. As a matter of fact, he would just as soon take his shower this minute and go home.

But the coach had him go back in. "Break the game loose," the coach said. "Nobody's doing anything out there except kicking the ball."

Jabber tossed aside the jacket, reported to the ref, and took Pat's place the instant there was an out-of-bounds kick.

He felt stiff. Those few seconds he had warmed up at the sideline, waiting for his chance to go in, were hardly enough to work the stiffness out of his joints.

But it didn't take long. A short pass to him from Stork gave him an opportunity to dribble the ball down the field and across the center line. When a couple of Blue Jacket players came tearing after him, he gave the ball a tremendous kick that sent it more than halfway down toward the Blue Jackets' goal line.

Break the game loose? The coach must be kidding! After the lousy day he had had, he couldn't break anything loose!

It's the old con game, Jabber thought. He's trying to build up my confidence. Well, I only wish it were working.

But as he ran down the field, he felt better as the

stiffness worked out of his joints. His energy flowed back into him. He became fresh and strong again.

Joe Sanford received the ball and booted it toward the goal area. Jack stopped it and tried to kick it in, only to be thwarted by a Blue Jacket full-back who gave the ball a hard enough boot to put it temporarily out of the danger zone.

It's the same old thing, thought Jabber. A score looks as if it's in the making, then the Blue Jackets drill it down the field. We're lucky we've got the points we have, he told himself.

The game soon ended, the score remaining Nuggets 2, Blue Jackets 1.

11

Jabber made his decision. Right or wrong, he felt it was the wisest step to make. He'd put the wallet back where he had found it. It was the only way he could make certain that Pete wouldn't accuse him of stealing it, and the money that was in it. Maybe Pete would find it on his way home.

He would do it now, after the game.

He finally reached the spot, recognizing the bush where his headache had begun. Glancing up the street and then behind him, assuring himself that no one was close enough to see him, he removed the wallet from his pocket and tossed it toward the bush. It fell open like a floundering butterfly. He left it like that and walked away.

He hadn't gone more than five steps when the

gravity of what he'd done hit him like a ton of bricks. Stupid, he thought. It was just stupid dropping the wallet back into the bush. It was infantile, ridiculous. And the act of a coward.

Sure, a coward. But would he be brave enough to give the wallet to Pete?

He'd wait and see. At the moment, he'd retrieve it. First things first.

He went back, picked it up, and had started to put it into his pocket when a car stopped along the curb beside him and a voice called his name.

"Hey, Jabber? What did you find?"

He almost froze. He hadn't thought of looking back to see if a car was coming this time. He hadn't heard it approach.

He looked at the driver. It was Tony Dranger, Pete's hang-gliding friend.

"Oh, hi, Tony," he greeted the other boy numbly. He could have crept into a hole.

"What was that? A wallet?" asked Tony.

Jabber nodded.

"Anything in it?"

Jabber opened it, his fingers trembling. "It's empty," he said.

"Any name in it?" asked Tony. "There should be an ID card in it somewhere."

Jabber looked at the ID card that stood staring him in the face.

"It's Pete's," he said.

"Whose?"

"Pete's. My brother's." Jabber's voice almost cracked.

"Well, how about that?" exclaimed Tony. "The one he lost while we were playing touch football. Wait'll he hears the sad news."

"Right," murmured Jabber.

"I was just going over to the house," explained Tony. "Want a lift?"

Jabber got into the car and rode the short distance to the house. Tony said something about asking Pete to go hang-gliding with him, but the words were just fuzzy sounds in Jabber's head. He was wondering how to face Pete when the showdown came. Now that Tony had seen him pick up the wallet, his decision to tell Pete the truth was a big step closer.

Tony parked in front of the house and started to get out. "Tony, just a minute," said Jabber.

He was breathing hard.

"Yes, what is it, Jabber?"

Jabber's face was hot. "Do me a favor, will you? Don't tell Pete about the wallet. Okay?"

"Oh, sure. You'd rather tell him yourself. I understand."

"Thanks, Tony."

They got out of the car and walked up the front steps. Jabber tried to open the door. It was locked. He pounded on the panel three times with the heavy brass knocker. In a moment the door opened, and Karen stood there.

"Oh, hi!" she said, her eyes brightening as she saw Tony. "Look what the cool air brought in!"

"Hi," said Jabber, going past her. With Tony behind him, she probably hadn't seen him, anyway.

Tony not only had a fondness for hang-gliding, he had recently developed a fondness for Karen, too. Jabber suspected that sometimes his coming to visit Pete about their favorite sport was just an opportunity for Tony to see her.

They talked in the living room while Jabber went

into the kitchen, where the aroma of hashed brown potatoes and hamburgers filled his nostrils.

"Hi, Mom," he said.

She looked at him from the table where she was reading the evening paper.

"Hi, son," she said. "We were waiting for you. How come you came in the front way? You usually come in the back."

"Tony Dranger's here. He picked me up. Is Pete home?"

"He's in his room. Better call him. Dinner's about ready."

He walked up the stairs and knocked on Pete's door.

"Yes?" came Pete's voice.

"Pete. Can I come in a minute?" asked Jabber.

"Sure. Come on."

He opened the door and went in. Pete was sitting on the bed, reading a magazine.

"Well, hi," he said amiably. "I knew you'd be coming home any minute. My stomach was throwing me signals. Who won?"

"We did. Two to one."

"Good for you. Any goals?"

"One." Jabber closed the door quietly behind him.

"What's the matter?" asked Pete, sliding his feet to the floor. "You're looking at me as if I'm a ghost."

"I'm sorry." Jabber took a deep breath and let it out slowly. "Pete, I've got something to tell you."

Their eyes locked.

"You found my wallet," said Pete, no emotion in his voice, no sparkle in his eyes.

Jabber's face paled. "How did you know?"

Pete's eyes lit up now. He smiled. "You mean I hit it on the nose? My wild guess was right? You really found my wallet?"

Jabber nodded. "Yes. I found it a couple of days ago. But I was afraid to tell you."

"Why?"

"I thought you'd accuse me of taking the money that was in it."

Pete's smile faded. "You mean that you found the wallet . . . empty?"

"That's right."

Pete looked at him squarely. It was hard to tell what he was thinking.

"You believe me, don't you?" said Jabber.

"Of course I believe you," said Pete. "Why shouldn't I?"

He got off the bed and started to pace up and down the room.

He doesn't believe me, thought Jabber. I knew he wouldn't.

"Where did you find it?" Pete asked.

"About half a block up the street. Near a bush. Pete, it's the truth. You've got to believe me. That's where I found it, and it was empty."

Pete paused. "About half a block up the street? I know I didn't lose it there."

"You said you lost it while playing touch football. Somebody must have found it, taken the money, seen your address, and tossed the empty wallet into the bush not far from where you live."

Pete's eyes crinkled. "How about that? You've got it all figured out."

The sharpness of the remark stung Jabber. He stared painfully at his brother. "Pete, trust me, I didn't take your money," he repeated, his voice rising. "The wallet was empty. Would I have picked it up and brought it to you if I had stolen it?"

He was breathing faster. Sweat glistened on his upper lip.

"Who's accusing you of stealing it?" said Pete. "I'm not. I just can't figure out anybody taking the money and dumping the empty wallet near our house, that's all. It doesn't make sense."

"I know what you're thinking," exclaimed Jabber, his throat aching. "You're thinking that I stole your money and used it to buy my soccer shoes. Would you think I'd pull a dirty trick like that?"

Pete stood silent. Jabber knew that his brother was thinking hard, weighing the evidence against him.

"No, Jabber," replied Pete. "I wouldn't think you'd pull a dirty trick like that. As a matter of fact, I think you showed a lot of guts bringing that empty wallet to me."

"You mean that, Pete?" Jabber wasn't sure whether to believe Pete or not.

"Of course I mean that," said Pete, smiling and thrusting out his hand.

Jabber shook it.

"Thanks, Pete." He felt as though a heavy weight had been lifted from his shoulders. Pete really sounded sincere. "Come on. Dinner's ready, and Tony's waiting to see you."

12

There were chores to be done early on Saturday morning before Pete and Jabber could leave for hang-gliding. The garbage had to be bagged. The lawn had to be cleaned of the tiny branches that had broken off the two willow trees during the heavy wind the previous night. The lawn had to be mowed, and right after breakfast a hole had to be dug for a magnolia tree Mrs. Morris had purchased from a nursery. She had been wanting to do it for days. Jabber knew it, but wished she had forgotten about it. He and Pete had dug a dozen holes for trees for their mother over the past two years, and hole-digging wasn't his idea of fun. Besides, most of the trees still looked like spindly sticks.

But Mrs. Morris had her heart in her plants, trees,

and flower garden, and didn't mind when the boys chided her about them.

Both their father and mother had loved the garden. Since their father had died she had continued taking care of it herself, not minding it because she loved it so, and because, she had once admitted to the children, it kept her "close to Dad."

Jabber thought it was a bit silly of her, but didn't say so. If she was happy with that thought, let her be.

Tony drove up at noon, his hang-glider strapped to the roof of his car.

"We haven't eaten yet," said Pete, when Tony came to the door.

"I brought some sandwiches and a Thermos jug of hot coffee," said Tony. "I thought we'd eat at the hill."

"Hey! You're thinking, man!" cried Pete. "Got enough for the three of us? Jabber's coming, too."

"Got plenty," answered Tony. "Besides, I had my mother stick an extra half a loaf of Italian bread and a hunk of salami into a bag. You ready?"

"In that case, we're ready!" said Pete, laughing.

The conversation in the car on the way to Knob

Hill touched on a sensitive topic for Jabber. It surprised and embarrassed him. It was Tony who brought it up.

"I heard that you might quit soccer and play football, Jabber," he said. "That true?"

He looked at Jabber in the rearview mirror, and must have noticed the surprised expression come over the younger boy's face. The sudden confusion.

"I said that?" said Jabber, frowning.

When? he wondered to himself. When did I say a thing like that? And to whom?

Then he remembered. He had said it to Mose Borman at the soccer game. In a fit of disgust. Oh, man!

Pete turned in the front seat and looked at him, his eyes brightening. "Hey! How come I hadn't heard of this?" he demanded.

Jabber smiled weakly. How could he tell Pete that he hadn't really meant it? That it was just something he had said off the top of his head?

"Where did you hear the scuttlebutt, friend?" Pete asked Tony when he received no answer from his brother.

"Mose Borman. Jabber's friend."

Mose ought to be hung, thought Jabber. I just said that because I was disgusted for playing so lousy. Why didn't Mose keep his mouth shut?

"Smart move, Jabber!" exclaimed Tony. "As a matter of fact, I was surprised you went out for soccer instead of football. After the big name your father made for himself I couldn't see for beans why you went out for a different sport. Right, Pete?"

"I've been telling him that all along," said Pete. "Hey, man, I'm pleased! This is good news!"

He extended his hand, and Jabber found himself shaking it. He felt in a dreamlike state. Why am I doing this? he asked himself. I don't want to play football! I want to play soccer!

On the other hand, Jabber saw how happy it had made Pete to think that he had changed his mind. And, if there were a lingering doubt in Pete's mind about Jabber's stealing his money, Jabber's shift to football would undoubtedly erase that, too.

"You tell Mom about this and she'll be happier than if you got her a hundred plants and flowers for her birthday," said Pete. "She's always wanted both of us to follow in Dad's footsteps in football, you know."

"She really likes football that much, does she?" asked Tony.

"Likes it? She never missed a game Dad played in," replied Pete enthusiastically.

"Does she go to your games?"

"Well, no. She doesn't have the time. She works all week, and on weekends she washes clothes, cleans up the house, et cetera, et cetera. Even with all of us helping out, my mother's a real busy woman."

She could find the time to go if she wanted to, thought Jabber. But if she went to see Pete play, she would have to make the time to see me play. It would be easier on everybody if I played football.

As they approached Knob Hill they saw a hang-glider already in the air. It was shifting briskly. Either the pilot was new at the controls, or the wind was unusually strong.

They drove up the hill and parked a few yards away from the only other car there. A girl was leaning against its front bumper, watching the hang-glider with more concern than interest. She glanced briefly at the newcomers, then shifted her attention back to the glider.

"That's Jane Wallace," said Tony. "And that's Tom

Miller flying the wing. He's not bad, but that wind is giving him a rough time. What do you think, Pete?"

"I've flown in stronger winds than this," replied Pete boldly. "Anyway, if Miller isn't scared, we're not going to chicken out, are we?"

Tony shrugged. "Okay."

The wind was changeable and stronger than any Jabber remembered experiencing before when he and Pete had come here to hang-glide. Deep inside he wished Pete would reconsider. But he knew his brother. Pete was fearless, proud. If Tom Miller was brave enough to hang-glide in this wind, Pete would be, too. Tony was just obliging Pete.

They removed the hang-gliders from the roof of the car, opened them, harnessed themselves, and prepared for flight.

"You first," said Tony.

A grin played across Pete's face. This was a sport he loved as much as football. He ran a short distance down the steep hill and took off. Instantly the strong wind caught the underside of his wing and carried him quickly up fifty feet.

Jabber's heart leaped as he stared frantically at the

yellow wing, at Pete strapped in it, and his dangling legs.

He shifted his attention to Tony. Tony hadn't moved. He looked worried. Already Pete was having a rough time.

"He shouldn't have gone," exclaimed Jabber. "I knew he shouldn't have gone. But you can't tell him that. You can't tell him anything. Better not go, Tony. That wind is too strong."

Pete was circling wide over the hill some two hundred yards away, his wing dipping and rising like a ship caught in a wild, tumultuous sea.

Jabber looked for Tom Miller, saw him down in the valley, gliding in for a landing. He heard clapping and a soft cry of triumph, and saw the girl, Jane Wallace, standing away from the car and applauding happily.

He glanced back toward Pete, and froze as he saw Pete's wing skimming the tops of the pine trees in the distance. Suddenly the yellow wing swooped toward the ground, rose for an instant, then floundered like a wounded bird.

In a moment Pete was on the ground, obscured by the wing.

"Tony! He's probably hurt!" shouted Jabber anxiously.

"Let's go!" said Tony, quickly releasing himself from the harness and folding the wing.

They sprinted across the rugged hill toward Pete, Jabber panting with worry. The wing was moving, billowing like a boat sail in the gusty wind. But Pete was lying still on the ground.

They reached him, and saw the look of pain on his face as he lay there, a hand clutching his left leg.

"Pete!" Tony crouched beside him.

"I think I busted my left leg," said Pete. "Oh, man, it hurts."

"The closest house is down in the valley," said Tony. "I'll drive down there and phone for an ambulance. Don't move. Just stay put."

He took off like a sprinter in a hundred-meter dash.

Jabber knelt beside his brother. "You shouldn't have tried it, Pete," he said, choking with emotion. "You saw the wind blowing Tom Miller around the sky. It was too strong."

Pete raised his hand. Jabber took it, squeezing it tenderly.

"It's spilt milk now, Jabber," said Pete with a pained smile. "I know I shouldn't have gone. But I would have been all right if that wind hadn't caught me by surprise when I took off. It lifted me so fast that I hurt my right wrist. From then on I couldn't control the wing. I'm sure I would've flown it without trouble if I hadn't hurt my wrist."

Still the sure, arrogant Pete. Hating to admit to failure.

As the minutes passed while they waited for the arrival of the ambulance, Jabber's mind began to race. What if the injury was so serious Pete couldn't finish the football season? Where would that leave Jabber? Would it really clinch his decision to give up soccer and shift to football?

Right now it looked to him as if it would.

It took twenty-seven minutes from the time Tony made the telephone call till the time the ambulance arrived. One of the two medics apologized for the delay, saying that they'd been on another emergency when the call came in.

They examined Pete's legs carefully and found that his left leg was fractured. How seriously, only an X ray could tell.

They hustled him off to the hospital, Jabber riding along with him, Tony following in his car.

"It was a stupid accident," complained Pete. "It burns me to a crisp."

"Maybe it's not too serious," Jabber said, trying to comfort his brother. "Maybe you'll be flying again before you know it."

"Well, it all depends," said Pete. "If I'm a fast healer, I might be back up on that hill tomorrow."

He laughed, and Jabber laughed with him.

"Don't bet on it," said the medic sitting beside Jabber.

It took only minutes before the ambulance, siren going, rolled up to the curb in front of the emergency entrance of the Birch Valley Hospital. Pete was rushed inside to the emergency ward where a doctor and a nurse were waiting for him. Carefully the medics moved him from the stretcher to a table.

"I'll call Mom and tell her," said Jabber.

"No. Wait a while," said Pete. "Maybe I won't have to stay here."

He lay stiffly, his eyes shut with pain.

"He your brother?" the doctor asked Jabber.

"Yes."

"Then why don't you sit in that office? The girl will want to ask you for some information. The hospital will need it for its records."

"Okay."

Jabber entered the office and sat down. The girl

across the desk from him smiled. "Hello," she greeted him amiably. "Can I help you?"

Jabber wet his lips nervously. He felt hot and uncomfortable. He had never been in a hospital before, except when he was born, and he certainly couldn't remember that.

He heard footsteps beside him, and felt a wave of relief as Tony Dranger came alongside him. With Tony as moral support, he had little difficulty from then on in answering the questions that the girl posed to him as she filled out a hospital form.

Two hours later, his leg in a cast, Pete was lying in a bed in Room 214 on the second floor. There was another bed in his room. A man was in it, sleeping soundly.

Jabber was there with his mother, Karen, Uncle Jerry, and Aunt Doris.

"Talk about lousy luck," grumbled Pete, sitting up in bed. "There goes football for the rest of the year. And the season's hardly started."

"You have no one to blame but yourself," said

Karen, sitting on the edge of the bed. "The wind's been blowing hard all day. You shouldn't have risked flying that wing."

"My other mother," snorted Pete. "Listen, I've flown that wing in stiff winds before. One of those gusts just caught me by surprise, that's all."

He crossed his arms firmly over his chest, and Jabber saw the tape around his right wrist.

"What about the wrist?" he asked.

"Sprained, just like I said," replied Pete.

"They tell you how long you might be in here?" asked Uncle Jerry.

"Two days at least," said Pete. "Maybe three or four. I don't know."

He sounded disgruntled, angry.

"Take it easy," said his aunt. She was a tall, stately woman with short-clipped, frosted hair and a warm, tender smile. "There have been lots of athletes who've had injuries much worse than yours, who came back and played in just a few short weeks. Don't take it so hard."

"Right," said Uncle Jerry. "Heck, it happens all the time."

He went on to tell how it had once happened

to him, and Jabber wondered if Pete was beginning to feel as he did. Listening to a pile of suggestions on how to ignore the despairing side of life and capitalize on its positive side was boring him to sleep.

Pete stopped the flow of platitudes with a raise of his hand. "If you'll pardon my interruption," he said, "Jabber's got some news for you good people. Tell 'em, Jabber."

Jabber stared at Pete.

"Go on," insisted Pete. "Tell 'em. Don't just stand there."

Jabber felt everyone's eyes focused on him. They waited, patiently.

Pete had him over a barrel. What could he say? He was trapped.

"I'm thinking of quitting soccer and playing football," he said, his heart pounding.

"Hey! How about that?" exclaimed Uncle Jerry. "It's about time!"

"Well!" said Mrs. Morris, her eyes widening. "And when did you decide to do that?"

"Probably when he found out that Pete had broken his leg," said Karen impudently.

Jabber blushed. "That's not so," he said, embarrassed. "I spoke about it to Pete and Tony on the way to Knob Hill."

"That's right, he did," vouched Pete. "But you said the same thing now that you said then, Jabber. You said you're *thinking* about quitting. Aren't you sure?"

Jabber met his eyes. "Almost," he said.

"Well, fine," said Uncle Jerry. "And on that happy note, what do you say we retreat? It's almost the end of visiting time, anyway."

Jabber was glad to leave. But in the car, on their way home, Karen hardly said a word to him. She was in front with their mother, who was talking about Pete and his foolish desire to fly hang-gliders; Jabber rode alone in the back seat.

"Someday he'll grow up and see how crazy it is," his mother said. "And I think you should quit it, too," she said over her shoulder to Jabber. "I know you're flying Pete's glider. You can't keep such secrets from me."

He forced a grin. "Nobody gets hurt if he learns how to fly those things well and is careful," he said.

"Careful?" she echoed. "What kid is careful about anything nowadays?"

She can go on and on talking about the skills and the hazards of hang-gliding, thought Jabber. Just as long as we keep away from the subject of soccer and football.

"It's your decision to make," Mose said as they headed for school on Monday morning. "I'm not going to try to influence you one way or another. Except that I *know* if you quit soccer to play football our future games will go *phttt!* Down the drain."

"Oh, no," said Jabber. "You're not trying to influence me one bit, are you?"

"Well, you asked me for my opinion, didn't you?"

"I did," agreed Jabber. "And I wish I hadn't. You've just made it tougher for me, that's all. The second time in a week."

Mose frowned at him. "What do you mean by that?"

"Why did you have to tell Tony Dranger that I said I was going to quit soccer to play football?"

"Why? Because you said it, that's why. You didn't tell me it was a secret."

"I was just kidding," said Jabber. "I didn't really mean it."

"Then neither did I."

Mose stamped hard on the sidewalk as if to give vent to his quick-rising temper without starting an argument. He was Jabber's best friend, but his boiling point was so low that even a provocative remark from Jabber could touch him off.

"Okay, forget it. I'm sorry," said Jabber. "Like you said, it's my decision. I'll figure it out somehow."

"We're playing the Blue Jackets on Thursday," Mose reminded him. "You'd better make up your mind by then."

"Suppose I don't?"

Mose looked at him. "With that load on your mind you wouldn't be worth a nickel. I know I wouldn't."

"Yeah," agreed Jabber. "You're right. Oh, man. You know, when I was a little kid I used to be proud that my father was a football star. Now, I don't know. I'm beginning to wish he hadn't been."

They walked the remaining distance to the school

without saying another word. Leaf shadows danced on their faces. A couple of kids biked by, honking their horns. Waving.

It looked like a nice day. But to Jabber it was lousy.

14

Tuesday came along, and Jabber still hadn't come to a decision. He hadn't promised anybody yet that he would quit soccer and play football. *Almost* was the word he had used in the hospital to Pete and the rest of his family. He had *almost* decided. That didn't mean that he had.

He knew that once he had made it, he was committed. He had to consider his integrity now, more so than ever before. Because he was older. Somehow, as a guy gets older, he becomes more aware of his responsibilities, his character.

The day dragged on, and by the end of the second period that afternoon he had made his decision. He'd drop soccer and play football. Nobody but nobody would be climbing up and down his back anymore.

Karen? Let her think what she wanted to. She'd get over it.

He would notify Coach Pike about his decision just before soccer practice that afternoon, he thought. Of course he didn't expect the coach to like it. But, so what? It's my life, reflected Jabber.

He went out to the field and stood by the bench in the cold, waiting for the team and Coach Pike to show up. He felt strange being alone, but he just couldn't face the coach in the locker room in front of all the guys. Their remarks to him, when they heard him tell the coach that he was quitting soccer for football, would make him wish he'd never been born.

By tomorrow they'd feel differently about it.

Maybe.

Anyway, he'd wait here.

He had been standing there about ten minutes, getting colder and colder, when Karen came riding up on her bike.

"Jabber!" she exclaimed, wide-eyed with surprise. "What are you doing here alone?"

"Waiting," he said.

"Waiting? For the team? Then you really have quit playing."

He shrugged, not answering.

"Pete wants to see you," she went on, her lips tightening into a straight line.

His eyebrows shot up. "Why? What's happened? Is he home?"

"No. He's still in the hospital. But he wants to see you right away. Uncle Jerry's waiting at home to take you."

He started running off the field and down the street, hearing the whirring sound of her bike chain as she followed him.

He got home and found Uncle Jerry peeling an orange in the kitchen. On the table there were a bag of oranges, a sack of potatoes, and a couple of cartons of eggs that he had brought.

"Hi, Uncle Jerry," Jabber greeted him, breathing hard from the long run. "Karen says that Pete wants to see me."

"Right. Say, that was quick. I figured you were either practicing soccer or football."

"Neither," said Jabber.

Uncle Jerry finished peeling the orange and

tossed the peelings into the garbage can. "Come on."

They started out the door.

"Aren't you coming?" Jabber asked his sister as he saw her opening the red sack and extracting an orange.

"No, thanks. I'll go up later with Mom," she said.

There was something about the way she looked at him that suggested she knew why Pete wanted to see him, and that she wasn't to be included.

What's on his mind, now? Jabber wondered. It must be important if he wants to see me.

"Hi, Jabber. Thanks for coming," Pete greeted him as Jabber entered the room ahead of Uncle Jerry. They shook hands. "Sit down."

Jabber sat on the edge of the bed, scanning his brother's eyes, wondering what was so important that Pete couldn't wait till tonight to tell him about it.

"I got a letter today, Jabber," Pete said, pulling out the drawer of the metal cabinet beside him and taking out a letter. "It's registered, and it's from a Mr. Vickers. Ever hear of the name before?"

Vickers? Jabber let the name roll around in his mind. It didn't ring a bell.

"No," he said.

"Look inside it," said Pete, handing the letter to his brother.

Jabber opened it. His heart leaped as he saw a sheaf of dollars.

"It's the stolen money," explained Pete. "Mr. Vickers found his kid with it, had him confess where he had gotten it, and mailed it back to me. Every dollar of it is there. Now, that's an honest man if I ever found one."

Jabber was tongue-tied, his eyes shiny as he looked long and hard at his brother. This was proof! he thought. Proof that he hadn't stolen Pete's money!

"I knew you still wondered if I believed you or not," said Pete. "And I did. I always did. But this absolves you completely. I knew it would take a load off your mind. That's why I wanted to tell you about it as soon as I could."

He opened his palm and Jabber, smiling happily, slapped it gently.

"One other thing," went on Pete. "I've had a lot of time lying here to think about things, especially about you. I spoke my piece to Uncle Jerry, too, so this won't surprise him. As a matter of fact, he agrees with me, and you know your uncle. He isn't the easiest guy in the world to make change his opinion."

Jabber grinned at his uncle. "I know," he said.

"Anyway," said Pete, "I've realized what a phony I've been about trying to make you do what I want you to do. I've been wetter than a soaked sponge, Jabber. I've had no business telling you what to do. I mean, just because Dad was a football star in college and then in the pros, why should you try to copy him? Know what I mean?"

Speechless, Jabber stared at him.

"What I'm saying, Jabber, is for you to do your own thing. You're a fine soccer player. So don't let Mom, or me, or Uncle Jerry, or anybody else tell you what sport to play. Okay?"

Jabber's heart flipped. There was an overcast sky outside, but it suddenly seemed very sunny in the room. A bird flew onto the windowsill, shrilled a few notes, and flew off.

"Thanks, Pete," he said. "That's all I needed. I'm going to stick to soccer."

"I thought you would," said Pete. "And don't worry about Mom. She'll see the light, too."

"And I have," admitted Uncle Jerry. "And as your brother intimated, I'm a stubborn critter. As for Karen, she's always been on your side, anyway."

"I know," said Jabber.

For the first time in days he felt free of the heavy burdens that had been plaguing him.

But not entirely. Regardless of what Pete had said, their mother's feeling would continue to bother Jabber. As of now, though, his future in sports would remain in soccer.

The Blue Jackets were tough, especially on their home field. For the first three minutes of the game they had possession of the ball most of the time, threatening to score twice except for the spectacular saves by Tommy Fitzpatrick.

"Way to go, Tommy!"

"The old fight, boy!"

But how long would Tommy be able to master the situation before he got tired and lost some of his zip?

"We've got to sock one in, Jabber," Mose said to him as they came up alongside each other. Al Hogan had just accepted a throw-in and was dribbling it up the center of the field.

"We'd better shoot for two, Mo," said Jabber, "before these monkeys really break loose on us."

"I'll go along with that," Mose said, grinning.

He ran up the field, watching Al evade a tackler with clever footwork. But, as another Blue Jacket player swept in toward him, Al booted the ball. It arched over Jabber's head. Both he and Mose sprinted after it, then headed straight across the center line as they saw Pat O'Donnell come in and stop the ball with his chest.

Two Blue Jackets swarmed upon Pat, but he got the ball off before they were too close. Mose trapped it with the inside of his thigh, dribbled it a couple of yards, then pushed it to Jabber.

"Take it, Jabber," he said. "And let's move it."

"Run ahead of me," advised Jabber.

Mose did, glancing now and then over his left shoulder. But a Blue Jacket, apparently noticing the setup, sprinted briefly toward Mose, then slowed down.

Clever, old boy, thought Jabber. But I'm not so dumb myself.

"Jab!" exclaimed a voice from his left side.

He saw Stork sweep past him, long white legs pumping. Jabber pushed the ball forward, a yard . . . two yards. As long as he wasn't challenged he'd dribble the ball.

Pounding feet sounded behind him. He booted the ball straight ahead. Stork got it, but could advance it only a few feet before a Blue Jacket man was on him, too.

Stork kicked aimlessly.

"Oh, watch it, Stork!" cried Jabber, speeding after the bad kick.

The ball struck the ground, bounced high, came down, and was met by a Blue Jacket fullback who jumped up a yard and headed the ball. Jabber, trying to halt his forward momentum, skidded and plowed into another Blue Jacket player, feeling as if he had run into a brick wall.

Stars exploded in his head. Standing still, he waited for the dizziness to leave him, the stars to disappear.

"You okay, Jabber?" Mose asked, stopping beside him.

"Yeah, I'm okay." He straightened up, looking for

the ball. "We blew our chance, Mose," he said disappointedly.

"Maybe," said Mose. "Jack's got the ball."

Jabber glanced across the field just as Jack Sylvan booted the ball from under the nose of a Blue Jacket player. Jerry Bunning, playing left wing, caught it and moved it deeper into Blue Jacket territory before he had to get rid of it.

Jabber broke down the field. "Mo! Keep to my right!" he called.

"Right!" said Mose.

Mike caught the pass, then almost lost it to a Blue Jacket halfback as they both fought for control of it.

"Here, Mike!" yelled Stork, running up behind the two players.

Mike pushed the ball aside with the instep of his right foot, getting it completely out of his opponent's way, then pushed it gently over to Stork. Stork got it and started to dribble it.

"Here, Stork! Here!" exclaimed Jabber as he saw the two Blue Jacket fullbacks attacking.

But still Stork didn't pass.

"Stork! What're you waiting for?" shouted Jabber. He was almost furious. Now was the best time they could have for a shot at the goal. Couldn't Stork see that?

Suddenly Stork stopped, using the instep of his left foot to stop the ball, too. Quickly he got between it and the two attacking Blue Jacket players. And Jabber, staring dumbfoundedly at him, wondered if Stork had lost his foolish mind.

Simultaneously, someone plowed into Jabber. A leg got between his two, tripping him, sending him crashing to the ground. He rolled over to prevent bruising his legs, and came up quickly to his feet again, just as a whistle shrilled.

"Foul!" shouted the ref, pointing a finger at the Blue Jacket offender.

Jabber glared at his opponent as he brushed himself off.

"Direct free-kick," announced the ref as he picked up the ball and tossed it to Jabber. "Right there, son. Where he ran into you."

Jabber caught the ball, set it on the ground, and stepped back.

"Make it, Jabber," said Mose. "Boot it in."

Jabber ran a hand across his forehead, scooping away a thin layer of sweat.

He heard shouts from the few fans bunched together near the Birch Central bench.

"Score, Jabber! Score!"

Karen's voice. Good ol' Karen. He hadn't seen her when the game had started. She must have arrived afterward.

He got ready to kick.

15

Running forward, Jabber aimed the ball directly for the middle of the goal where the Blue Jackets' goalkeeper stood crouched, waiting.

He reached the ball, timing his approach accurately. But instead of kicking it in its center, he struck it with the inside of his foot, driving it like a shot to the left of the goalie.

The goalie sprang after it — but too late.

Goal!

"Thataboy, Jabber!" Mose shouted, patting him on the back.

"Great kick, Jab!" cried Stork.

From the bench, and from the fans, came cheers, too.

Birch Central had broken the 0–0 tie.

✿   ✿   ✿

The first part of the second quarter was almost a repetition of the first. The Blue Jackets fought like conquerors. Jake Henderson, their hard-playing center, seemed to be all over the middle of the field — running, kicking, meeting the ball with his head, his knees, his feet. He had one thing in mind, to get the ball into Birch Central's goal.

They were approaching the Birch Central penalty area, the Blue Jackets still in control, when Jabber noticed a strategy in the making.

Jake was dribbling toward the goal. From his left a Blue Jacket forward was moving in, slowly, as if trying to avoid attention.

Eddie Bailor, helping Tommy protect the goal area, ran after Jake, either to take the ball from him or to force him to kick. Jabber knew that Jake wouldn't kick the ball straight toward the goal. For one thing, he was too far away from it to make a certain goal. For another, Eddie was in the way.

Jake kicked the ball with his instep to his left forward, and instantly Jabber saw the intent of the play. Jake had purposely drawn Eddie out of his position so that he, Jake, would be free to move in.

Jabber ran ahead, maintaining a distance just a

few feet to the left of Jake. He stifled a wry grin as he saw the surprised expression come over the left forward's face. The kid, about to kick, hesitated, then kicked anyway.

Instead of Jake, it was Jabber who stopped the ball with his chest, dribbled it a few feet to get it in position, then kicked it hard upfield where Jerry was waiting for it.

"Hey, man! Nice play!" said Stork as they ran down the field together.

Jabber grinned. "Couldn't see any sense letting them tie up the game," he said.

"Right!" Stork laughed.

Jerry pushed the ball aside to Mike, who dribbled it downfield a short distance, then booted it to Jack. Jack lost it as Jake pounced in like a springing tiger, controlling it for a minute, then kicking it back downfield.

Again it was a tug-of-war, the ball getting closer and closer to the Nuggets' goal.

"Get to that ball and kick it back upfield!" Jabber yelled. "Let's get it outa here!"

"Yell your head off, Jabberoo," exclaimed Jake

haughtily. "This time we're gonna put that ball down your throats!"

Jabber could tell by the determined look in Jake's wide, piercing blue eyes that he meant it.

"No way, Jake," he answered. "No way."

He said it, but he lacked the conviction that Jake had.

A half passed the ball to Jake. Jake dribbled it in, crossing into the penalty area and getting into position for a kick. This time he was going to try it himself. No strategy stuff. He was going to make sure.

Jabber saw his intention and charged him. Jake, a cocky kid, had to be thwarted somehow. There was only one way to do it that Jabber could think of at the moment.

"Watch it, Jake!" he yelled as he rushed toward the tall center.

For a fraction of a second Jake turned his head, then drew back his foot to kick. But that brief hesitation seemed to be all that was required to throw his aim off.

His foot met the ball off-center, slicing it low and

to the right, missing the goalpost by two feet and rolling across the goal line.

Phreeet! shrilled the ref's whistle. "Gold out!" he yelled.

Jabber met Jake's darting eyes as the Blue Jackets' center kicked angrily at the sod and turned away.

"Sorry about that, Jake," said Jabber amusedly.

"It ain't over yet," Jake replied.

Jabber grinned. He seldom needled an opposing player, but when a player needled him first, he welcomed the opportunity to throw some of his own darts.

The half ended a few minutes later.

Resting on their benches during the ten-minute intermission, the Nuggets listened avidly to Coach Pike as he pointed out their misplays, and advised what to do if the same situations arose again. They knew that this was the one game where they needed all the help they could get. The coach didn't talk very long, but what he said stuck in their minds.

"Oh, Jabber," Mose said, while they waited for the remaining minutes to pass. "Any news about your brother's wallet?"

"Oh, sure. He got it back. And the money, too."

"He did? No kidding! The cops catch the crook or what?"

"No," said Jabber. "A kid did it, and the kid's father found him with the money. He made the kid confess, then mailed the money — every cent of it — to Pete."

"Who was the kid?"

"Vickers. I don't know his first name."

"Rollie or Ronnie, something like that," said Mose. "I know of him. He's a wise guy."

The coach glanced at his watch. "Let's get on the field," he said. "The second half will be starting in a few minutes."

The team rose off the benches, some of the members slower than the others. They were getting tired.

"What do your mother and Pete think about your decision to stay with soccer?" Mose asked as he and Jabber trotted onto the field.

"It was Pete who changed his mind about my playing," explained Jabber. "I guess he had plenty of time to think about it while he was resting in the hospital. I don't know about my mother. I still don't think she likes the idea, and I'm afraid it hurts her.

But it's my life, Mose. If my father chose to play football, why can't I choose to play soccer? I guess she has trouble understanding that."

"Yeah," agreed Mose. "I suppose it is hard for her to come to grips with a thing like that."

Reminding Jabber of his mother made him glance toward the Birch Central fans sitting in the small grandstand. He recognized Karen's red sweater and blue hat. Next to her sat Pete, who had come home yesterday from the hospital. And next to Pete — Jabber cut his stride, and stared — sat a woman wearing a beige leather coat and a matching hat. Even from that distance he recognized the round face, the gentle slope of her shoulders. It was his mother.

The Nuggets threatened during the first three minutes, maintaining possession of the ball most of the time in enemy territory. It was only a matter of seconds, Jabber was sure, before they'd pop in their second score.

But the tide changed. A mad scramble for the ball in the Blue Jackets' penalty area resulted in a long kick by a Blue Jacket fullback that sent the ball flying down the field, aided by a wind that had been slowly picking up.

Jake Henderson received it and propelled it deeper into Nugget land. Jabber, Mose, and Mike sprinted down the field, Jabber dismayed at the sudden turn of events. Goes to show, he thought, that you can never be sure about anything.

A Blue Jacket wing took a pass from Jake and booted it to his left forward, who subsequently passed it back to Jake.

The goal shot was quick, clear, and sure — shooting past Tommy's outstretched hand like a bullet.

Nuggets 1, Blue Jackets 1.

"What did I tell you, Jabberoo?" said Jake, a wry grin crossing his face.

"You said you'd do it, and you did," replied Jabber calmly. "But as you also said, the game isn't over yet."

It was in the fourth and final quarter when apparent bad luck struck the Nuggets. Al Hogan pushed a Blue Jacket wing just as the player was about to kick the ball, a foul so obvious that everyone watching the play could see it.

Phreeet! went the whistle, and the player was given a direct free-kick.

"Man, did I blow it," exclaimed Al. "I ought to kick myself."

"Just hope that he doesn't make it," said Jabber, fighting the temptation to tell Al what he really thought about such a stupid move.

The ball was placed on the spot where the penalty occurred. The Blue Jacket player got into position to kick. The Nuggets' defensemen lined up in front of the goal like a blockade.

The player kicked to a forward running in toward the goal. At the same instant Al burst forward, blocking the kick as the forward booted it. The ball ricocheted to Eddie, who kicked it hard up the field where Mose and Jabber were waiting for it.

Mose got it, passed to Jabber. Jabber kicked it across the center line to Stork, then raced down toward the right side of the goal, no one coming near him.

Screams rose from the Nuggets' fans as Stork passed the ball to Rusty. Two defensemen double-teamed him, but he got the ball away from them — pushing it gently to one side, then booting it in the path of Jabber Morris.

Straight ahead of him was the goal. Only one player stood between it and him. The goalkeeper.

Jabber kicked. The ball sprang off his foot like a stone leaving a slingshot. It headed for the open space just inside the right goalpost.

The Blue Jackets' goalie leaped for it, but missed it by a yard. Goal!

Nuggets 2, Blue Jackets 1.

Cheers exploded from the bench and the fans.

"Nice shot, Jabber!" cried Mose, slapping his buddy on the back.

Jabber met Jake's hard glare. "There isn't much time left, Jake," he said.

Jake said nothing.

As it turned out, there really wasn't much time left, and the game went to the Nuggets.

They shook hands with each other — then the Nuggets shook hands with the Blue Jackets, after which both teams headed for the school.

"Javis."

Jabber heard the familiar voice and turned. His hot face widened into a broad smile. "Hi, Mom," he said. "How did you like the game?"

She was with Karen, smiling happily, proudly. "I liked it very much," she said. "You were good. As a matter of fact, you were the best. But I wasn't surprised."

"You sure it's all right, Mom?" he asked her.

"Of course, it's all right," she said. "Am I such a fool that I can't see how selfish I was? But don't you think the game is rough?"

"Rough?" Jabber echoed in surprise.

Karen laughed. "Leave it to her to worry about that!" she exclaimed.

"Not any rougher than football, Mom," said Jabber. "See you later. Hot dogs and sauerkraut for dinner?"

His mother's eyes sparkled. "With ketchup," she answered, still smiling as he took off for the locker room.

READ ALL THE BOOKS
In The
New MATT CHRISTOPHER Sports Library!